# First Fence

For more information, visit nzponywriter.com

Email nzponywriter@gmail.com and sign up to my mailing list for exclusive previews, new releases, giveaways and more!

Pony Jumpers
#1

# FIRST FENCE

Kate Lattey

1st Edition (print).

Cover image from iStock photo.

ISBN-13: 978-1539837831
ISBN-10: 1539837831

- ♥ -

It's not about the social accessories,
the money, the ribbons.
It's not about the winning; that comes easy.
It's about the horse: how to care for the horse,
how to ride the horse,
and how to look after this great animal -
the horse.

*George Morris*

- ♥ -

# 1

# SQUIB

My bike skidded across the dirt, spattering my jodhpurs with flecks of mud. *Goodbye turnout points*, I thought sadly as I leaned my bike up against the tin shed at the edge of the Pony Club paddock. Our head coach was a stickler for correct and spotless turnout, and week after week she tutted over my patched and stained jodhpurs, which refused to look clean no matter how many times I washed them.

I dragged the shed's reluctant door open, and checked the time. Twenty minutes behind schedule. Of course today had to have been the day that my bus got stuck in traffic after school, which meant I'd had no time to grab a snack before changing into my Pony Club uniform and biking down here as fast as I could. I scrambled over the fence and walked across the big paddock, halter swinging from my fingertips as I scanned the ten-acre paddock for my pony.

Mud sloshed around the edges of my jodhpur boots as I headed towards his most likely location, down in the gully where there was still a bit of grass at the tail end of winter. I felt the cold water seeping into my sock as I walked, and the buckles of the halter I was carrying clinked merrily. But although I was late, squelching through the mud, and the mist sitting low over the hills was hinting at more rain to come, I couldn't help smiling. I was on my way to catch my pony, and although I'd had him for almost a year now, it still seemed like a dream sometimes, that my parents had finally bought me a pony of my own. Mum and Dad had no interest in horses, and couldn't understand why I wasn't happy with hockey or soccer, why I couldn't play a sport that they understood and that didn't involve the complete care and responsibility of another life. But I'd worn them down eventually, escaping to the local stables every weekend to ride, earning my lessons through hard work, and eventually my family had realised that I wasn't going to outgrow my horse-madness after all.

The ponies came into view ahead of me, half-hidden in the trees at the bottom of the gully, and I walked down the slippery hill towards them, casting my eyes across our small herd. Cobber, the solid chestnut with a big white blaze, and gangly dark bay Duke were both grazing on the side of the hill. A small bright bay pony with a bushy forelock and a white face peeked out from behind a tree, and a slender roan pony was standing close behind him. They were Oscar and Rebel, and either their young owners weren't coming to our Pony Club rally today, or they were running even later than I was. I found that slightly comforting as I kept looking around, and finally saw Squib.

More accurately, I saw his butt. He was standing in a thick clump of flax bushes, with just his rump and tail sticking out towards me. My grin at the sight of him faded when I saw the dark brown streaks in his white tail, and I groaned. He was about to make my filthy jodhs look clean in contrast.

I heard a shout from behind me, and Squib's head flew up as Carolina came running towards us, her skinny legs flashing in bright pink gumboots.

"Oscaaar!" she cried, her shrill voice carrying across the paddock.

Her little bay pony raised his head an inch from the ground, still chewing, and observed her calmly. Carrie's sister Alyssa trudged along behind her, dragging her own halter and being chivvied from the gate by their mother Sandra as Rebel gave his rider a wary look. They hadn't owned the sensitive roan pony for very long, but he was already giving nervous Alyssa palpitations every time her mother legged her into the saddle.

Squib had backed out of the flax bushes and was staring at the commotion, his ears pricked right up and his big dark eyes bright. I could read the mischief on his face as he watched Carrie run up to Oscar and fling her arms around his neck. Her small pony didn't flinch, just kept eating while his young rider attempted to halter him with his nose still on the ground.

I chirruped to Squib and he looked at me, muscles still tensed beneath his dark grey coat. I dug quickly into my pocket for something to tempt him with, but there was nothing there except a scrunched-up tissue. *Better than nothing. Maybe he'll be fooled.* I held it out, trying to kid him into believing that it was a piece of bread or apple, but Squib was no fool. With a snort and a toss of his head, he spun on his heels and trotted away from me. My heart sank as I watched him bound into a canter, kicking up his heels as he passed Alyssa and delighting in her shriek of alarm before taking off across the paddock in a thunder of hooves, daring me to try and catch him now.

By the time I finally did get my hands on Squib, I was well and truly late for Pony Club. I'd spent a good fifteen minutes following my bucking, farting pony around the paddock, until Sandra had got sick of watching. She'd marched into our small tin shed and thrown a handful of her pony nuts into a bucket, then rattled it at Squib as he raced past her. Skidding to a halt, my pony spun on his rounded quarters and trotted towards Sandra, looking as though butter wouldn't melt in his mouth. With his head in the bucket, he was easy to catch, and when I finally got him haltered he led back to the gate as gently as a lamb.

"You should leave a halter on him if you're going to have that much trouble catching him every day," Sandra scolded me as I latched the gate behind us, chivvying Squib sideways with a poke at his round side.

"I don't want it to get caught on the trees," I replied.

I'd read that warning in the Pony Club Manual, and there were a lot of low-hanging branches in our paddock. I'd rather take half an hour to catch my pony every day than come down one afternoon to find him hanging from a tree, but before I could tell Sandra that, she'd scurried off to finish grooming Alyssa's pony for her, because her daughter was having another of her tantrums and was refusing to touch Rebel's quivering coat. Carrie was sloshing copious amounts of hoof oil onto the ground as she attempted to polish Oscar's hooves, blithely ignoring the large piece of manuka stuck in his tail or the big patches of dried mud on his hindquarters.

I tied Squib up with a quick-release knot and went to fetch my tack. The corner of the shed that held my gear was spartan compared to everyone else's. Sandra had never been a rider, or even a horse person, but she'd thrown herself whole-heartedly into being a Pony Club mum, and her daughters had enough tack between them for a dozen ponies. Their gear was always spilling out of their area and encroaching on my small space, so before I could even get to my corner I had to move one of Carrie's bright pink buckets out of the way. It overflowed as I lifted it, scattering brushes and baby wipes and bottles of tail conditioner, plaiting bands and mane combs and some weird-looking grooming tools that I didn't even recognise, let alone have the first idea what they'd be for. I was pretty sure that nine-year-old Carrie didn't either, but if it was for sale at a tack shop, Sandra would buy it, and so their collection grew.

I picked up Squib's small bucket of brushes, which I'd bought a cheap bulk lot when I got him last year, and slung his second-hand Wintec saddle over my arm, unable to stop myself from giving it a critical look. The girth had cracks along the plastic edges, my stirrup leathers didn't match, and the Velcro on Squib's banged-up tendon boots barely stayed closed anymore. But I smiled in brief satisfaction as I picked up his bridle and slung it over my shoulder. I'd saved up all winter for it, and it had been worth every penny. Soft brown leather with a padded headstall, plaited reins and a grackle noseband with a fuzzy bit of sheepskin in the middle. It made him look really flash, and the noseband helped me to keep him under control a bit better, although most of my control still went out the window when he was faced towards a jump.

Jumping was Squib's favourite thing in the world – aside from food, that is. He'd attack any obstacle with gusto, bounding towards it with his head in the air, flinging himself sky high and kicking up his heels as he landed. I couldn't be sure whether the adrenalin I got from it was excitement or sheer terror, but we almost always ended up on the other side, so at least we weren't a total disaster.

Or so I'd thought. By the time I got Squib presentable and tacked up, the rally was well underway, and I was reprimanded for my lateness by the head coach Donna.

"It's not as though you've got far to come," she told me, reminding me that I grazed on the adjacent grounds and only had a thirty-second ride to get to rally. "Some of our members live half an hour away, and they're always on time."

I wanted to tell her that their parents probably didn't work night shifts or have a sister who needed constant supervision, but she was already waving me towards a group of riders in the far corner.

"You can join in with Deb's group. She's here as a favour to us today, so be respectful and try to keep that mad thing under control," Donna said, casting a doubtful glance at Squib.

I turned him away, and he bounded forward, squealed at a small pony who was coming too close for his liking, pretended to buck, then trotted off towards Deb's group with his nose in the air.

"Mad," I heard the coach saying behind me, and I knew she was shaking her head. "I'm telling you, that pony's a menace."

The woman named Deb was standing in the middle of a group of riders, all circling around her at a walk. I rode Squib into the middle of the circle and managed to halt him right before he flattened her.

"Sorry I'm late."

Faint lines appeared around Deb's eyes and mouth as she smiled at me. She was middle-aged, probably in her forties, with dark hair in a short ponytail and a gorgeous orange windbreaker that I immediately coveted.

"That's all right, hun. What's your name?"

"AJ. And this is Squib."

My pony pricked his ears and did his best to look cute and likeable as Deb rubbed his forehead. It seemed to work, because her smile broadened as she looked him over.

"He's very cute. How old? Have you had him long?"

"Six. And I've had him for almost a year. He doesn't know much," I admitted. "But he's a really keen jumper."

"That's what we like to hear. Join into the group behind Katy," she told me, pointing to a girl I'd never seen before on a gorgeous flaxen chestnut pony.

I let Squib jog out onto the circle and reined him back to a walk behind the chestnut. The pony swished his immaculately clean tail, his round hindquarters rippling with every step of his long, flowing stride. His coat gleamed, his mane and tail were perfectly pulled and his low socks were blindingly white. We picked up a trot, and I watched his rider, sitting tall and appearing to be doing nothing at all, her hands still and her legs immobile as her pony flexed gently at the bit. *Oh, to be able to ride like that. To have a pony that well-schooled...*

"Canter on," Deb said and the chestnut pony stepped smoothly into a supple, active canter. Squib pulled at the reins and followed, tossing his head as I fought to keep him from crowding the other pony's heels.

"AJ, sit up and half halt him," Deb called to me.

I wasn't quite sure what a half halt was or how to do one, but I tugged at the reins so it would look like I was at least doing something. As usual, Squib did the exact opposite of what I wanted him to, grabbing the bit and charging into the chestnut pony's hindquarters.

Katy turned her head and shot me an annoyed look as her pony sidestepped nervously. I quickly apologized, struggling to control Squib as Deb told us to come back to a trot. The chestnut pony transitioned smoothly back down, and Squib seized his opportunity to win what he had decided was a race, and cantered a full lap around the circle of riders before I could convince him to return to a trot.

"Keen, isn't he?" Deb asked me with a smile, unfazed by my pony's bad behaviour.

Usually by now, Donna would be screaming at me to get Squib under control, and half of the time she would make me go away and school him by myself in the corner, which only ever made Squib crazier and harder to control, but I suppose it meant she didn't have to watch.

But Deb didn't do that. Instead she had everyone else walk while I cantered on the other rein, giving me her full attention as Squib careened around her in ever-decreasing circles.

"Sit up AJ, use your seat. Bring him back to you. Half-halt."

I tried again, pulling sharply on Squib's reins for a moment before releasing, and he did slow down a little bit, but I could sense Deb's consternation.

"Hang on. Come back to walk for a moment. Katy, pick up a canter and show her what I mean."

I hauled Squib back to a jog, which was the closest I could get to a walk out of him, and watched as Katy's pony glided effortlessly into a canter, straight from the walk. He stepped through from behind, his neck was arched and eyes bright, and she was beautifully balanced in the saddle. Everything looked perfect to me, but Deb somehow found things to correct.

"Lift your hands a bit, get that inside hind leg working," she called. "Now ride him forward."

Once again, Katy's aids were imperceptible. Her pony's stride lengthened and sped up slightly, and as she cantered past me, Deb called to her to half-halt, telling me to "watch how she does it".

I did my best, but other than the fact that Katy sat up a bit straighter, I couldn't see her doing anything. Her pony responded immediately though, his canter slowing down right away.

"And again, collect him up more," Deb called, and again I saw nothing except the response Katy got from her pony. Perhaps a slight movement of her hands, but little else.

"Okay, back to walk, give Lucas a pat," Deb told Katy, then turned back to me. "See that?"

I went for total honesty. "I saw the response. I didn't see how she did it."

Deb turned towards Katy. "Want to explain your aids?"

Katy twisted in her saddle and looked over her shoulder at me. "Sit up, sit back, close your seat, close your hands."

She recited the aids fluidly, sounding bored by the elementary nature of it, then swung back around in her saddle to face forwards. As though riding correctly it was just that easy to do, and took no effort at all.

Deb encouraged me to try again, and I heard Jessie start complaining that if we spent the whole lesson trying to get Squib under control then we'd be there for literally hours. I ignored her and picked up the reins, then nudged Squib into his fast canter. Deb called instructions to me, and after a moment of confusion, I realised what she meant for me to do, and tried it. *Sit up, sit back, close your seat, close your hands.* This time, it actually worked. Squib steadied his stride and slowed down slightly, although his canter got bouncier, making him even harder to sit on than usual. But for a moment there, for just a moment, I felt a surge of power from his hindquarters propelling us along. It was the kind of canter that you wished could last forever, the kind that would take you over a metre-twenty oxer without even blinking.

Of course, it didn't last. Within a few strides, Squib was scurrying along at high speed again and ignoring me, and I had to turn him in small circles to get him to slow back to a trot. I clapped his sweaty neck and praised him as Deb moved on to coach the rest of our group. Once they'd each managed to canter a circle, we moved on to jumping.

One by one, everyone trotted over the crossbar, then cantered over the vertical. Katy looked bored beyond belief, her pony doing everything perfectly while the rest of us struggled. Jessie's pony ran out at the vertical, Ashley's skittish young Thoroughbred knocked both jumps down, and James's elderly roan pony ran out of impulsion and dribbled to a lazy halt in front of the second fence. Squib, meanwhile, flung himself over both jumps with huge enthusiasm, clearing each one by miles and nearly throwing me out of the saddle.

As I circled him around, trying to get him back under control, I noticed that Katy was watching me. She looked interested for the first time that day, as Squib did his best to drag my arms out of their sockets.

"He can really jump!" Deb called to me as Jessie came back around for another attempt at the low fences. "Stand over there with Katy for a minute while I get these guys through."

Katy's eyes were still on me as Squib sidled towards her beautiful pony, but she didn't look as annoyed at me as she had before. But she didn't say anything as Squib sniffed noses with her chestnut, then laid his ears back and squealed.

"Squib! That's rude," I told him, and Katy shrugged, a half-smile appearing on her narrow face.

"It's okay. Lucas is paddocked with mares, he's used to it."

"He's gorgeous," I told her, unable to tear my eyes away now that we were close up.

His copper coat gleamed with good health, his neatly pulled mane lay evenly on one side of his muscular neck, and every inch of both him and his tack was spotlessly clean. Squib's mane could never decide whether to lie on the left or right, so it split the difference and changed over halfway. I knew there were still manure stains on his hocks and in his tail, and his hooves needed to be trimmed again, but I was having the devil of a time getting the farrier to return my phone calls. At least his bridle looked good.

"I like your pony," Katy said.

I shot her a suspicious look, wondering whether she was making fun of me. Nobody really liked Squib, because he was so naughty and difficult to control. Even the coaches who said that he showed potential as a jumper thought that I was stupid to have bought him, and kept saying that I should sell him and buy something more experienced. But I loved my pony, and I knew he could be a superstar one day. I certainly wasn't going to sell him to someone else and let them have all the glory.

"Thanks. I like yours too. Is he a good jumper?"

Katy nodded. "Yeah, he's not bad."

I looked across at the other riders, who were now cantering fairly competently over the line of jumps, which had been raised to about eighty centimetres, with an oxer added at the end.

"Are we going to get to jump again, do you think?"

"Yeah, Mum's just waiting until these numpties are done and then she'll put the jumps up for us."

It clicked into place then, and I wondered why I hadn't seen it before. "Deb's your mum."

They looked so similar that it was ridiculous of me not to have realised. Same dark hair, same slender build, same light brown eyes and high cheekbones. Same air of calm competence, although Katy had a reserved edge to her that her friendlier mother didn't seem to share.

I watched Deb set up a third fence and send the others down the line again. Squib shifted his weight restlessly, and Lucas flickered an ear at him.

"I haven't seen you at rallies before," I commented, and Katy shrugged.

"We only come at the start of the season. Got to get the

rallies in so we can get into team events. But we don't bother after that because it's so much standing around, and if I wanted Mum to teach me she could do it at home." She sighed, and patted Lucas's rump. "I wish she'd hurry up though. I've got three more ponies to work and an English assessment due on Friday that I've barely even started. Finally!"

Katy sat up and nudged Lucas forward as Deb waved us over. I shortened Squib's reins as he followed his new friend, and soon we were cantering down the line of jumps. Squib was as speedy as ever, but when Deb put the jumps up higher he had to slow down to avoid crashing through them, and I felt a little more under control.

Down the line we went, and up went the jumps until the oxer at the back was immense. Lucas was jumping flawlessly, so Deb told Katy to cross her stirrups and do it with her arms folded. I thought she was joking, but Katy obeyed, barely moving in the saddle as her pony soared effortlessly over the jumps without any guidance from her.

"Your turn," Deb said to me, and I swallowed hard.

"I don't know what he'll do if I don't have the reins," I admitted, and she laughed.

"You can keep your reins and stirrups! I'm just trying to make life a bit harder for Katy. You just go down as normal."

I was relieved to hear it, though there was nothing normal about the height of that last jump, which looked huge from where I was sitting. Still, if Katy could do it without stirrups or reins, surely I could do it with the benefit of both.

Squib's blood was up and he cantered excitedly to the crossbar, flinging himself over and racing the two strides to the vertical. Deb yelled to me to sit up and hold him, and I did my best as we made the three strides to the oxer. Squib never flinched at the height, seeming to view it as a personal challenge, and he flew over easily. I was grinning as we landed, but not for long. Squib was so thrilled by his own efforts that he gave himself a victory lap, pulling the reins out of my hands and launching into a series of triumphant bucks.

I was thrown from the saddle, and as the grass came rushing up to meet me, all I could think before I hit the ground were two simple words.

*Worth it.*

# 2

# NOT FOR SALE

Dax was barking as I walked up the driveway, and I quickly let myself into the house, ruffling his ears and telling him to shush. I could hear my family in the living room, my sister Alexia's voice carrying as always as she yelled at Dax to shut up. She loved our dog as much as the rest of us, but she couldn't handle his loud bark, or any other loud noises - with the notable exception of her own voice.

"Sorry I'm late," I said as I went into the room with Dax panting on my heels.

Everyone was sitting around the dining table – everyone except Mum, of course, who was working late as usual. There was a big bowl of spaghetti bolognaise in the middle of the table, and I quickly sat down in the empty chair next to Alexia and started to fill my plate.

She wrinkled her nose. "You stink."

"Eau de horse," Dad said with a smile. "How was Pony Club? Did Squib behave?"

Anders made a disparaging noise, and I shot him a dirty look as I added salad to my plate.

"He did, actually. Well, he bucked me off once but we

jumped some really big jumps. There was this girl there called Katy, and she's a really good rider. And her mum was coaching, and she was super helpful. She said that Squib…"

"Can I be excused?" Alexia asked abruptly, interrupting the flow of my conversation.

"Not yet," Dad said calmly. "AJ's only just started eating."

"But she's late. It's not *my* fault that she's late." Alexia pouted at him, slapping her cutlery down onto the table irritably.

"I don't mind," I said quickly, sensing a storm building, but Dad held firm.

"No. We wait until everyone is finished before we leave the table," he reminded her.

"Don't worry Lex, at the speed she eats we'll be out of here in no time," Anders said comfortingly, but Alexia just slumped back in her chair with a sulky expression.

"You were saying?" Dad asked me.

"Don't make her talk, she'll just take even longer to finish eating," Anders told him, with a wink in Lexi's direction. "Besides, nobody actually cares what her pony did today."

I kicked my brother under the table, but he moved his leg and I got the chair leg instead. As I winced at the stabbing pain in my toe, Anders leaned back on his chair and grinned at me.

"Serves you right."

"I hate you."

"That's not very nice," Astrid piped up from the other end of the table. "You shouldn't hate anybody, right Dad?"

"That's right, Chicken."

I shovelled more food into my mouth as Dad looked at me again, so he diverted his attention to my eldest brother, who was finishing off the spaghetti I'd left behind.

"Do you have a game this weekend?"

Aidan nodded. "Saturday morning. Anders is playing in the early afternoon, so we'll go together." He looked at Anders. "Which means an early start for you, bro."

"I live for early starts," Anders assured him.

"You'll sleep the whole way there and back again," Aidan replied. "Good thing I still don't trust you enough to drive."

As Anders started trying to defend his driving ability while everyone else reminded him of the long list of dents and prangs and speeding tickets he'd already picked up in his few short months of driving, I scoffed down the rest of my dinner, well aware of Alexia's eyes boring into me as I ate. My sister had never been any good at sitting still or waiting for other people, and her irritation could build into a tantrum really quickly. It wasn't her fault. *It's just how she's wired*, as Dad often reminded us. But I always did my best to keep the peace, and not set her off if I could avoid it. Alexia in full screaming mode was no fun for anybody, least of all her.

It wasn't until later that night, when I was doing homework in the study because Astrid had already gone to bed and we still shared a bedroom, that Dad got to finish our conversation. He always tried really hard to listen to all of us, perhaps more aware than we were of how much time and attention went into keeping Alexia copacetic.

"So." He sat down on the window seat and looked at me attentively. "You fell off, you said?"

"Yeah, but I'm fine." I appreciated his efforts to talk, but I was in the middle of a series of complicated algebra equations, and I didn't need the distraction. "No harm, no foul."

"Well. I'm glad."

Dad sat for a moment longer, watching as I concentrated on the work in front of me. I was almost done, but the next step was eluding me. I chewed the end of my pen, and Dad seemed to realise that his presence wasn't helpful. He slapped his hands onto his knees, then stood up.

"Don't stay up too late."

I shook my head. "I'm almost done."

"Okay. Good night, Possum."

Always with the nicknames. Sometimes I wondered why he'd bothered giving us proper names at all, since he never used them. The answer to the equation leapt out at me then, and I quickly scrawled it down. *Done.*

"Night Dad," I said, but he'd already gone.


"Hey, AJ! Wait up!"

I turned to see Katy walking towards me, her schoolbag slung over one shoulder as she shoved her way through the crowded hallway. Her hair was tied back in a messy ponytail, her school shirt was crumpled and her socks sagged around her ankles. It took me a moment to recognise her as the perfectly polished rider I'd seen at Pony Club only the day before.

I stopped and waited as she caught up. "Hi."

I hadn't expected her to talk to me – we didn't exactly move in the same social circles. Although I wasn't really sure which social circles she was even a part of. But I smiled at her and she shot me a brief smile in return as we made our way out into the sunlight.

"Would you consider selling your pony?"

I was so surprised that I stopped walking, until an older boy rammed into me from behind and swore at me, prompting me back into motion. Katy had paused to wait, and when I caught up with her again I shook my head emphatically.

"No way. He's not for sale."

Katy looked disappointed. "Shame. He'd make a super Grand Prix pony. Is that your goal with him?"

"Um…"

I hadn't ever really thought about that. Competition was something we did when we got the chance, but we didn't have many of those. And getting Squib under control had always been my first priority, with the idea of competing a very distant second. The way he behaved right now left a lot of room for improvement, and Donna had told me more than once that I had a lot of work to do before he was safe to take out in public on a regular basis.

"Not really," I told Katy. "I don't compete much."

She looked at me as though I was crazy. "Why on earth not? Competing is the best part of riding."

I bit my tongue for a moment before I responded. "Well, we don't have a float, so I can only go to shows that are within riding distance, or sometimes I get a ride with people from Pony Club. But it's hard to find people who want to take Squib because he's not very good at loading."

That was a nice way of putting it. Squib's aversion to horse floats had started last year when he'd baulked at going onto Donna's float, after she'd reluctantly agreed to take me to a mounted games day. I'd wanted to stop and let him take his time, but we were running late so Donna had taken over, trying to bully him into it. Half an hour later, a trembling Squib was finally in the float, but he'd travelled badly, behaved terribly at the show, and it had taken almost two hours to get him on again to travel home. Since then, I had always had to allow at least an hour to get him loaded, and sometimes it took more than that. Not surprisingly, it was pretty difficult to get people to volunteer to transport a naughty pony who was a devil to load and kicked the sides of the float the whole way there and back.

"That's easily fixed though," Katy said with a shrug. "You should've seen what Robin was like when we got him. Just stood at the bottom of the ramp and dug his heels in. But Mum did a ton of work with him on the ground and got him really good, and now he goes in by himself without even being led."

I looked at her hopefully. "Could she help me with Squib, do you think?"

"Sure, why not? It's not that hard. You just have to get their trust and respect on the ground. Helps for when you're in the saddle too." She stopped at the next block of classrooms and pointed towards the Art room. "I'm in here now. What're you doing tomorrow?"

"Um." I thought quickly. "No plans."

"You should come over. Bring Squib. You can ride to ours, it's not far." She gave me quick directions. "Any time. If you come over in the morning you can help me work the ponies. I've got far too many at the moment and they all need ridden at this time of the year. I'm trying to get Mum to put Robin on the market, but she's holding back until he's got a few more ribbons to his name." She rolled her eyes. "I cannot wait to get rid of that useless lump. He's honestly the most boring pony ever." Her eyes lit up suddenly. "You can ride him if you want."

I raised an eyebrow. "Wow, you're really selling him to me," I said sarcastically.

Katy grinned. "Fair enough. We'll flip a coin or something. You'll come though, right?"

I nodded. I had no other plans for the weekend, and getting some help with Squib sounded wonderful. "Of course."

"Awesome. See you tomorrow. Any time after ten or so is fine. Bye!"

And she turned and hurried into school without a backward glance.

# 3

# GROUNDWORK

Squib was excited to be going somewhere new, and he tossed his head and yanked at the bit eagerly as I turned him down the road that Katy lived on.

"Simmer down," I told my pony as his hooves danced along the edges of the sealed road. "Don't dislocate my shoulders before we even get there."

I'd woken early that morning, putting on my cleanest jodhs and the smartest polo shirt I owned. Katy might be scruffy at school, but I knew that her standards of turnout for her ponies were extremely high. I'd gone down to the paddock early, and since Squib had actually let me catch him on the first attempt, I'd had time to scrub the grass and manure stains off his hocks and even wash his tail, which was now hanging damp and stringy between his back legs. His tack was as clean as I could get it and he had his best purple saddle blanket on, which I usually reserved for shows.

I counted the numbers on the letterboxes as Squib spooked and bounded along the road, unable as usual to walk like a normal pony. *Why behave sensibly when you can impersonate a carousel horse?* had always been his motto. The road seemed to stretch on forever, and I was very happy to finally see the white post and rail fence and green letterbox that Katy had told me to look out for. A quick glance confirmed that the number was correct, and I turned Squib down the pine-edged driveway and let him trot on. His eyes popped out of the sides of his head as he made his way down at a springy trot, propping and spooking at invisible monsters as he went.

On the last bend, a bird flew out of the low bushes next to him and he properly spooked this time, shooting forward with his head in the air. I lost a stirrup and even if I hadn't, I knew I couldn't stop him. When he dropped the bit like that and ran off on me, all I could do was hold on and hope he'd settle down again soon. Donna always told me to pull him in a tight circle, but that only worked when you had room to turn, and I didn't. Plus, the last time I'd done that Squib had just about fallen over on top of me, a terrifying moment for both of us that I wasn't keen to repeat.

So all of my attempts at looking professional and respectable and not like a complete muppet were utterly destroyed by Squib as we came careening around the corner sideways with his nose pointing at the sky, and my lost stirrup swinging around and hitting him in the flank. And any hope I'd had of managing to get him under control before anyone noticed was quickly squashed, because he skidded straight into the middle of a small yard where both Katy and her mother were standing.

Katy was sitting on the back of a gorgeous bay pony, the reins slack on its neck as she chatted with her mum, who was fussing with the pony's bridle. They spun around and stared at me as Squib bolted towards them, and Katy's pony snorted and backed up swiftly, eyes wide.

There was barely enough room to turn Squib, but I had to try, so I grabbed at the left rein and pulled him away from Katy's unhappy pony as Deb jumped out of the way.

"I'm so sorry," I managed to shout over the clatter of my pony's hooves as I hauled him around.

Fortunately, the sight of another pony had piqued Squib's interest, and he was relatively easy to stop. He stood still at last, blowing hard as he stared excitedly at Katy's pony, then tossed his head and pawed the ground.

"Talk about your dramatic entrance," Katy said as she urged her pony forward, while Deb walked up to Squib and rubbed his head.

"Morning AJ."

"Hi. I'm so sorry," I said again as Katy's pony baulked at coming any closer to mine, which I couldn't say I blamed her for.

"Does he do that a lot?" Deb asked, looking carefully at Squib's snaffle bit.

My heart sank as I waited to hear the inevitable next comment, about how I should put him in a Pelham bit, or a gag, so that I would have more control. Except I'd tried both of those bits already, and they'd both made him worse. Besides, although I didn't know much about riding, I'd read lots of books on horse training and they all said that milder bits were better, and horses that were hard to control in gentle bits just needed more schooling.

"Have you tried him in a copper roller, or a Waterford?" Deb asked me, confirming my suspicions.

I shook my head. I had no idea what those bits were, but I

didn't really want to take him out of his snaffle.

"And at least a martingale. Stop him sticking his head all the way up and getting away from you," Katy added.

I looked over at her, and noticed that although her sleek bay pony was beautifully groomed, Katy was riding in dirty jeans and a t-shirt with a rip in one shoulder. Clearly her impeccable turnout was saved for public outings, and I felt a bit better about my own scruffy jodhs.

"We've got heaps of bits in the tack room, you can try something on him later if you want," Katy offered. "I've got to get Molly worked, but chuck Squib in one of the boxes for a bit, and we'll have a play with him later."

"Okay." I slid to the ground in embarrassed relief as Katy clicked her tongue at her pony and rode through a nearby gate into an arena.

"Just put him in here," Deb told me as she opened the door of a nearby loosebox, and I led Squib in behind her.

Their large outbuilding had a corrugated iron roof and walls, but the boxes were open at the front and sides, with wooden walls between them at human chest height. I took Squib's saddle and bridle off and he walked in a few circles, dug up some bedding, then charged to the front of the box and let out an ear-splitting whinny.

Katy's pony answered, and Deb shook her head. "She's not going to get any schooling done if Molly starts fretting. We'll bring one of the other ponies in to keep your boy quiet."

I felt my cheeks redden, and apologised again. "Sorry. He's such a pain sometimes."

Deb smiled at me. "He's just being a pony. None of them

like being all alone in a new place." She pulled a halter off a nearby hook and handed it to me, then pointed at the paddock next to the house. "Pop in there and grab Robin out, he's the chunky bay with the blue cover on. Whip his rug off when he comes in, then throw them a biscuit of hay each, give them something to do."

She motioned to the stacked bales of hay at the other end of the outbuilding before striding off to help her daughter.

As I caught Robin and put him up next to Squib, I couldn't help wishing that I'd grown up like Katy, with ponies on my back doorstep and a mum who knew all about riding and schooling and could fix all the ponies' problems. I stuffed the hay into the feeders, then discovered that Squib only had a third of a bucket of water, and Robin's was empty. After a quick scout around, I found the water tap on the side of the building, and filled both buckets up with the hose. It was a warm day, so I took Robin's rug off and gave him a quick flick over with a body brush that was sitting on the divider between the boxes. With both ponies happily munching on their hay, I wandered over to the arena and watched Katy cantering in smooth circles while her mum coached her.

"More inside leg, really ask her to bend through her ribcage."

Katy shot her mother an annoyed look. "I *am* using my inside leg."

"Well, you're not using it enough."

"Would you like to get on and do it better?" Katy snapped in response as she cantered past, and Deb threw her hands up and turned away.

She noticed me standing at the gate, smiled again and waved

me over. "AJ, could you give me a hand with these poles?"

Soon we had a bending line of three jumps built, with placing poles between each one, and Katy cantered Molly carefully down the line, then back the other way. Her riding still appeared flawless to me, but her mother had a few comments to make, most of which were met with eye-rolling from her daughter.

"She's still being a bit lazy behind," Deb said critically.

"So put the jumps up and give her something to think about," Katy replied, then looked at me. "AJ, can you put the middle one up three holes?"

I looked at the jump then back at her, wondering if Deb was going to contradict that instruction. The fence was already high, and putting it up three holes was going to bring it to around my shoulder height. But nobody seemed to think it was an outrageous request, so I walked over to the jump and lifted it at one end.

Deb walked over and adjusted the other side. "Put it up six holes and teach her a lesson."

She wasn't kidding, but then Katy called that she was coming and we moved to the sides of the jump as she approached. Molly cleared the first fence, cantered the three strides to the tall vertical, jumped it effortlessly and cantered on to the last, taking it in stride as well.

"Better," Deb said mildly as Katy brought her pony back to a powerful trot and shot a triumphant look at her mother. "Walk her off, then you can take Robin out for a hack."

Katy groaned and dropped the reins onto Molly's damp neck. "Do I have to? Can't AJ ride him? She said she wanted to."

That wasn't quite what I'd said, and we both knew it, but Robin had seemed like a sweet pony to me when I'd groomed him, and I was always keen to ride.

"If you want me to, I don't mind."

"Awesome!" Katy rode Molly through the gate and leaned down to grab a halter and lead off a nearby fence. "I'll go get Puppet, he could use an adventure."

She rode off down the raceway between their paddocks as Deb and I went back to check on the ponies. Squib had finished his hay already, and was leaning over the divider between the boxes, licking his lips and watching Robin methodically chew through his own rations.

Deb laughed at him. "He looks like he enjoys his meals."

"Food is all he lives for," I confirmed to her. "He'll do anything for a carrot or a bucket of feed."

"Speaking of that, Katy said you'd had some trouble getting him on a float," Deb said, stopping in front of Squib's box and rubbing his ears when he came over to say hi.

"Yeah, he hates it."

I explained what had happened with Donna that day, and Deb shook her head.

"One bad experience counts for a lot with horses. Being prey animals, they're genetically hard-wired to remember negative experiences where they feel as though their life was endangered, and it can take a long time to break through that barrier." My heart sank, but she smiled reassuringly. "I said a long time, not never. Wait there."

She went into the tack room, and came back with a rope halter and long lead rope.

"Let's pull him out and do a quick bit of ground work with him while we wait for Katy to get back," she said decisively, stepping into the box with Squib and knotting the halter onto his head, then leading him out behind her.

After a few steps across the yard she stopped, but Squib kept going.

"Hmm." Deb applied pressure to the lead rope, and Squib pulled against it, then turned in a half-circle around her before coming to a halt, his ears pricked forward as he faced her.

"Hasn't had much ground work, has he?" she asked as she went to Squib's shoulder and flicked the end of the rope towards him.

I knew what she was doing, because I'd seen people do it in YouTube videos. She wanted Squib to make a small circle around her, but he threw his head up instead and pretended he didn't know what she was on about, pivoting on his forelegs every time she tried to make him step away from her.

"Sorry," I found myself saying, and Deb looked over at me.

"Don't apologise. If you don't know something then you can't be expected to teach him. Grab Robin out of his box for a minute, and I'll show you what I'm trying to achieve."

When Katy got back, still riding Molly and leading a slender black pony off one side of her, I had Robin walking and trotting in circles around me on the end of the long rope. When I stepped towards him he would stop and turn towards me, and when I clicked my tongue and stepped to one side he'd walk off on a circle in the opposite direction. I could get him to back up just by walking straight towards him and if I walked backwards, he walked towards me, stopping as soon as I did. It was as though there was an invisible thread between us, and it was an amazing feeling. I started to appreciate just how much easier things would be if your pony was this attuned to you. I could imagine that if I walked up the ramp of a horse float right now, Robin would follow me in without hesitation.

Katy slid to the ground and rolled her eyes.

"More rope-twirling," she teased her mother, whose attention was focused on Squib.

"You only think it's a waste of time because I do it all for you," Deb told her daughter matter-of-factly. "If I didn't do all this groundwork with your ponies, they wouldn't be nearly as manageable as they are."

"If you say so," Katy shrugged, leading the ponies up to the boxes. She flipped the lead rope over the black pony's neck and slapped him gently on the rump as he approached Squib's open stable door. "Go on then, Pups. You know where the food is."

The pony walked willingly into the box and immediately started sniffing around in the corner for some hay, while Katy led Molly into the box next door to him.

"If you're done playing horse whisperer, I'll show you what tack to use on Robin," Katy called to me as I watched her mother work with Squib.

I was actually finding it all pretty interesting, but I wanted to ride Robin too, so I led him back to his box and shut him in again. Katy came out of Molly's stable with an armload of tack and kicked the door shut behind her.

"This way."

She led me down to the tack room at the end of the row of

boxes, and I looked around at the saddles and bridles neatly hanging from the walls. A big shelf on one side of the room held brushes, saddle blankets, hoof oils and all kinds of other things, and a row of large wooden pegs with covers hanging from them filled the far wall. Katy slung Molly's saddle onto a nearby saddle rack, yanking the damp saddle blanket out from underneath and throwing it into a pile on the floor.

"Mum needs to hurry up and do the laundry," she muttered. "Now, Robin." She grabbed a saddle and snaffle bridle down and handed them over to me, then added a girth and a faded red saddle blanket.

"Here you go. Match your shirt," she said cheerfully, before digging some bright red boots out of a box under the bridles and adding them to the gear in my arms. "Brushes are already out there somewhere. Go nuts with whatever you can find."

She turned away from me then and surveyed the wall of saddles with narrowing eyes. "Hmm, what will fit Puppy…" she said, speaking more to herself than me. "Maybe Forbes's saddle."

I had to ask. "How many ponies do you have?"

"Um. Six at the moment." She glanced at me as she turned to grab a bridle off the wall, and laughed. "Too many, really. I'm hoping to get some sold in the holidays, though as soon as I do Mum will just buy more. She can't help herself."

"How do you find time to ride them all?"

I had enough trouble fitting Squib in sometimes, what with school and hockey and netball, plus I had been considering getting back into competitive swimming this year. I mentioned this to Katy, and she shrugged as we walked out of the tack room, loaded up with gear.

"I don't really do anything else," she replied. "Just ride. Mum will usually lunge one a day, and they're all trained to pony off each other, so I can hack one out and lead another one which cuts it down big time. They all have Mondays off, that's recovery day from the shows. We go away competing almost every weekend."

It sounded wonderful, but crazy at the same time. "What about your social life?" I asked her. "When do you hang out with your friends?"

Katy slung the saddle across the wooden door to Puppet's box. "At the shows," she said, as if it was obvious. "I don't have any non-horsey friends."

I was surprised by that, though it did make sense. After all, if you were away competing every weekend, your friends back home were going to get pretty sick of hanging around waiting for you to spend time with them.

"What about over winter, when there aren't so many shows?"

Katy frowned at me. "What is this, twenty questions?"

"Sorry. I was just curious. I haven't really met anyone who competes so much before."

She shrugged as she unbuckled Puppet's fly sheet and pulled it off him. "I get as much schoolwork done as I can, so that I don't fall behind during the season. Because once the three-day weekend shows start, I don't really go to school on Fridays, but it's important to keep up. I've already passed most of my subjects this year, just need a few more Art credits and then that one will be knocked off as well."

I couldn't imagine my parents letting me skip that much

school, but I supposed that's what it took to get to the top. And I was starting to quickly appreciate just how close to the top of her game Katy really was.

# 4

# BITTED UP

"I don't get how you don't compete," Katy said as we rode Robin and Puppet out across their paddocks. "What's even the point of riding if you're not going to shows?"

"I just like riding," I said, feeling defensive. "And I'm not good enough to compete much anyway."

"Whatever," Katy said dismissively. "You ride fine and your pony is amazing. If I had a pony like him, I'd be taking him out every weekend."

"Yeah, well it's not that easy. Even aside from how hard it is to get him on a float, Squib goes a bit mental at shows."

"Does he do that running away thing on you?"

I nodded, and she looked thoughtful. "Let's try him in a copper roller this afternoon, and a running martingale. That might help."

I hesitated for a moment, then voiced my concerns. "But shouldn't I just work on schooling him more instead of using gadgets to get him to behave?"

Katy shot me an amused look. "Has schooling worked so far?"

"Well…"

"Look, I'm not saying you should tie his head to his chest

or put him in a double bridle or something. A copper roller's a good bit for a pony like him, it works pretty much like a snaffle but he can't hold onto it and run through your aids. And until you get him properly between your hand and leg, the martingale will help if he tries to throw his head up and run away from you. It doesn't mean you can't go back to milder gear later on when you've got more control, but not every pony is going to go perfectly in a loose-ring snaffle and cavesson noseband."

"Yours all do," I said, looking at the ponies we were riding. I couldn't remember seeing her ride in anything other than a plain snaffle on any of her ponies so far.

"Yeah, but they're all either babies or super established. Well, other than Mr Plod over there, but he doesn't have enough spunk to even try and run away or do anything bad."

I gave Robin a sympathetic pat as he ambled along beside Puppet. "He's a sweet pony," I said in his defense.

"He's fine, he's just boring. I like to have to work a little bit, you know? I've got him entered in the Show Hunters this weekend, I reckon he'll clean them up and then we can sell him to some uninspired kid who wants to canter slowly over eighty centimetre jumps for the rest of their life, and then I won't have to ride him ever again."

"Poor Robin. Why'd you buy him if you hate him so much?"

"Mum bought him, because she felt sorry for him. Believe it or not, he was skinny when we got him. Mum figured if we put some food into him he might liven up enough to be worthwhile, but you could pump him full of oats and he'd still just plod along. I'll show you. Let's canter."

She urged Puppet into a canter, and the young pony shot forward, throwing his head around for a moment before settling into his stride. Robin walked placidly until I urged him to follow, then cantered ponderously up the hill behind the black pony.

"I see what you mean," I told Katy as I kicked Robin along to the summit, where Puppet was waiting with his ears pricked. "He's not exactly enthusiastic."

"Nope, and he's exactly the same when he's jumping. I shouldn't complain really," she said as we walked the ponies along the ridgeline. "Ponies that are as dead to the world as him are actually worth a lot of money, because they're quiet and parents want them for their wimpy children. Once he's got a competition record, he'll be a cash cow and the money can all go into the fund to buy me a quality Young Rider horse."

"You're really lucky, you know," I told her as she leaned down to open a gate. "My parents aren't even interested in ponies, let alone willing to take me to shows."

"Yeah, what's up with that?" Katy asked, waiting for me to ride Robin through the gate before shutting it behind us. "Is your mum scared of horses or something?"

I shook my head. "Mum's a police detective. She's not much scared of anything. But I'm one of five kids, so really I'm just grateful that they bought me a pony at all."

"See, but you're the lucky one," Katy argued. "I hate being an only child. It's so boring, especially since it's just me and Mum. If we didn't have the ponies we'd probably have killed each other by now."

"Hmm, I guess. But this way you get all the time and attention.

And all the money spent on you," I added. "Everything we have has to be split between the five of us, though in reality most of it goes to Alexia, and we fight over what's left."

Katy turned in her saddle to look at me as Puppet led the way down the narrow track. "That sucks. Why's Alexia the favourite child?"

"She has Asperger's," I explained, wishing I hadn't brought this up. "It's a form of autism. So she struggles with some stuff, and my parents have had a really hard time keeping her in school, because although she's super smart she's kind of difficult to deal with sometimes, and none of our schools are funded enough to cope with it. So she gets a bunch of extra tutoring and special help and things. Mum works all kinds of crazy hours in her job, so Dad's usually running the household and the rest of us have just learned to be pretty self-sufficient."

Katy didn't say anything as the ground levelled out and she nudged Puppet into a trot, heading along a winding track between two hills. Robin meandered along behind and I urged him to keep up, watching Puppet spook and shy at silly things, just like Squib would. I never thought I'd be bored while riding, or miss my crazy pony, but Katy was right about Robin. He was dull as ditch water, and I couldn't wait to get back on Squib again.

Katy pulled up at another gate, and as I rode through it behind her, she asked another question.

"How old is your sister?"

"She's sixteen now."

"So you're the youngest?"

"No, Astrid's the youngest."

"Do you have brothers as well?"

"Yeah, Aidan's the oldest, then Anders is a year younger than him. And yes, I know it's weird how all our names start with A. Our parents never made it past the first letter of the alphabet."

"What's AJ short for?"

I pulled a face. "I'm not telling you. So don't ask."

"That bad, huh?" Katy grinned at me, and I shook my head in warning. "Fine, don't tell me. I'll find out some other way. So wait, Anders Maclean is your brother?"

"Yep."

"Wow. You're lucky. He's so hot."

I groaned. "Yuck."

"He is!" Katy insisted.

"He's my *brother*," I reminded her.

"Yeah, but that doesn't mean it's not true. Come on," she urged me. "You must be able to at least see it, from an objective standpoint. Like if someone showed you a picture of him and said *do you think this guy is hot*, you couldn't actually say *yuck*."

"Trust me. If you'd grown up with Anders, you'd know how disgusting he actually is," I told her firmly.

Of course I knew my brother was good-looking. Everyone knew it, including Anders himself, but that didn't make him any less of a pain in the neck to live with.

"You do look a bit like him," Katy said thoughtfully, reining Puppet back so that we were riding alongside each other, and studying my face. "Now that I think about it."

I pulled a face. "Gross, stop it. Come on, I'll race you back up the hill."

"Hah! You'll lose," she warned me, but I had already set my

heels to Robin's sides and pointed him up the slope.

Surprised, the bay pony leapt forward and started making his way up at a reasonable speed. I heard Katy shriek behind me, and was pushing Robin on faster when Puppet went streaking past – without his rider.

"What do you mean, you just fell off?"

Katy's mother looked unimpressed when we rode back into the yard half an hour later, both of us doubling on Robin as he trudged along. Puppet had jumped the fence at the top of the hill and taken himself back to the yard.

"You're lucky he didn't trip in his reins or flip over!" Deb scolded her. "He's not your pony Katy, you can't risk anything happening to him!"

"Settle down, he's fine. Right?" Katy asked as she slid off Robin and crossed the yard towards her pony, who was now shut in a box with his tack off, munching cheerfully on a pile of hay.

"It was entirely my fault," I said quickly. "I cantered off without warning her and he bucked her off."

At least, that's what Katy had said happened. I hadn't seen any of it until Puppet had passed me.

"Broke his reins, but nothing else, fortunately." Deb still looked mad, and I felt really bad about it. "You shouldn't gallop off in front of young ponies," she told me, and my face got hotter as I dismounted.

"She hardly galloped off," Katy interjected. "And Robin wouldn't know how to gallop, even if she'd tried to. It just took Pup by surprise, that's all. Besides, he's going to have to learn how to cope with someone falling off him if Lacey's planning on riding him in the future."

There was a bitter edge to Katy's voice as she exited Puppet's box and latched the door behind her, and I wondered who Lacey was.

"Yes, well. I'm sure he doesn't need that lesson quite so early on," Deb countered. "He's only been broken in for a couple of weeks, remember."

I felt even worse then. I hadn't realised how young and green the pony was – he'd behaved so well otherwise. Well, he'd been a bit spooky and daft, but that was normal behaviour to me.

"I'm really sorry."

"Oh stop apologising, nobody died," Katy said firmly, coming into Robin's box and taking his bridle off for me. "Don't worry about Mum, she just gets her knickers in a knot when the ponies come home without me because usually it means she has to get on the quad and go find me, and last time she did that she drove it off a bank and broke her arm. At least this time you were with me and she could just wait for us to turn back up."

I followed Katy into the tack room and put Robin's gear away. My stomach rumbled audibly as I hung up his bridle, and she laughed.

"Hungry? Me too. Let's go get some lunch before we deal to that nutter of yours."

Katy's house was small and untidy, with piles of clothes and junk lying all over the place. It was quickly becoming evident to me that the orderliness of their yard and the immaculate turnout of their ponies didn't reflect the way that she and Deb lived the rest of their lives. Not that I minded. It was much nicer to walk into a house that felt lived-in than one that was so clean and tidy that you didn't want to sit down for fear of making the couch dirty.

Katy scooped up a small long-haired terrier and cuddled it as she walked into the kitchen, while I was distracted by the photos on the walls, and the huge sashes and rosettes hanging above the fireplace.

"Wow. Did you win all these?"

"Mum sure didn't," Katy said as her mother came into the house behind us. "Those are just the big ones. I've got heaps more in my room."

"Glad to see I raised you with so much modesty," Deb said.

Katy stuck her tongue out at her mother. "Don't be jealous. Just because you live vicariously through my success."

"Nothing to do with the quality of ponies you ride, of course," Deb retorted.

"I haven't noticed any of them winning a Grand Prix without me on them," her daughter replied. "In fact, I seem to remember that Molly had never even been entered in a Grand Prix until I got her. What was it that Steph said, when she leased her to us? *She's no superstar, but she'll go well enough at the lower heights.* Proved *her* wrong."

"Enough," Deb said. "AJ is going to start thinking you've got a head the size of Australia in a minute."

Katy flopped down onto the couch and the little dog climbed up and licked her chin. "Get out of it Critter, you disgusting creature," she told it good-naturedly, while doing nothing to stop the assault.

"Are you going to the show tomorrow AJ?" Deb asked, and I shook my head.

"Duh, Mum. She has no transport, remember?"

"She could come with us," Deb said as she started slicing cheese off a block. "We'll have a space in the truck."

Katy shrugged. "That's true." She looked at me. "You wanna?"

"Um. Where are you going?"

"Just up the road to the sports day at Woodville. There's nothing much there, a few little classes. Nothing worth taking the good ponies too, just a few rounds for the babies. But it'd be good mileage for Squib."

"I'd love to, but I don't know if he'll go on your truck," I admitted.

"We'll try him this afternoon, see what he does," Deb said cheerfully. "Katy, find her a programme and let her have a look at it."

Moments later, I found myself balancing a plate of grilled cheese sandwiches in my lap and flicking through a show program, trying to look nonchalant and not as though I was overflowing with excitement at the thought of going to a show. Katy sat on the arm of the couch and leaned over me, then jabbed a finger at the page.

"You could do the ninety class as a warm up, then the metre round and the metre-five speed. That's the same as what Forbes is entered in."

I swallowed. "I don't know if we can jump that high," I told her.

"What? You jumped him a good metre-ten at Pony Club the other day. Wouldn't it have been, Mum?"

"Closer to a metre-fifteen, by my reckoning," Deb said as

she sat down next to me, half on a pile of laundry that covered most of the couch. "Your pony has the scope easily, and he doesn't look to me like he'd be a stopper."

I shook my head. "He's never refused."

"There you go then," Katy declared. "What've you got to lose?"

*Just my life.* "Nothing, I guess." I looked from one to the other, then back down at the programme. "If you think we can do it, then sure. If he goes on the truck."

"Oh, he'll go on. Don't worry about that. Getting ponies on horse trucks is Mum's area of expertise. Trust me," Katy said, swiping the last sandwich off my plate. "He'll be loaded up before you can blink."

# 5

# HELPING HANDS

It wasn't quite that quick, but within the space of half an hour, Deb had Squib leading confidently up and down the ramp of their horse truck, and a few minutes after that, she shut him in and walked away.

"It's a miracle."

I stared up the ramp at my pony, standing calmly in the truck and munching on the small pile of hay she'd left in there as a temptation.

"It's horsemanship," Deb told me. "Once I had control of his feet, he was quite happy to let me make other decisions for him. Fortunately, I don't think he's been so much scared as annoyed by his previous experiences, and the truck is a bit more open and inviting than a float, which probably helps too."

"All right then, let's get him off now so that AJ can ride him," Katy said. "We still have to try him in the copper roller, so that hopefully she'll have some brakes at the show tomorrow."

The copper roller bit looked similar to a normal snaffle, except that the mouthpiece had small copper pieces built in that rotated when I rolled them between my fingers.

"Will it hurt him?"

"It's not barbed wire," Katy told me. "If you don't like how he goes in it, then feel free to go back to your snaffle. Just give it a shot."

"Okay." I looked at the martingale that Deb was adjusting to fit my pony's broad chest, and told myself that it would be fine. These people knew what they were doing, after all. Far more so than I did.

Katy put Squib's bridle on and adjusted the grackle noseband. "At least you've got the common sense to tie his mouth shut," she commented, grinning when I winced.

"We'll help you school him more so you can ride him without this gear," Deb assured me calmly. "Once he's properly between your hand and leg, and balanced and supple and through, then you can start minimising gear. But there's no point riding without any brakes and then having to haul on his mouth or risk your own life when you go galloping full tilt towards the jumps because you have no way of stopping."

I nodded, her words making sense despite my reservations.

Katy huffed impatiently. "Just get on and ride him, and if he goes no better or worse, then you can go back to riding him in the mildest bit imaginable and just praying that he behaves himself."

The annoying part was, they were right. As soon as I started riding Squib, I discovered that when I took a hold on the reins and told him to stop, he actually did it. If he threw his head in the air, the martingale rings that connected to the reins put pressure on the bit, making him lower his head again. It still felt a bit like cheating, but within twenty minutes of schooling under Deb's expert guidance, Squib was trotting and cantering almost like a normal pony. He wasn't as balanced or consistent as Katy's ponies, but he was a lot better than he ever had been before. And he wasn't rearing or running away from the bit, like he had in the gag, or slamming on the brakes every time I touched the reins like he had in the Pelham.

"Told you," Katy said in satisfaction after I had jumped cleanly down the line of three jumps (significantly lowered from their previous height, but still bigger than I'd usually have jumped) and been able to halt afterwards with minimal fuss.

And when Katy put the jumps up even bigger, and Squib got excited and tried to buck, I could get his head back up and stop him before he got me off.

"It's like magic!" I exclaimed as I patted my pony's neck, and Katy and her mum both laughed.

"Witchcraft," Katy said, cracking her knuckles.

"It might as well be," I agreed. "Thanks so much. I'll definitely have to get one of these bits."

I hoped they wouldn't be too expensive, since I didn't have a lot of money saved after buying Squib's bridle.

"Don't worry about it, just use that one in the meantime," Deb said with a casual flick of her hand. "We're not using it, and I think there's another one in the tack room somewhere." She looked at her watch. "Crikey, we'd better get a move on if we're going to get those ponies washed before tomorrow."

"Speak for yourself," Katy said, getting to her feet from where she'd been sitting on an oil drum, her tiny dog cradled in her lap. "I've still got three ponies to ride."

"And I'd better head home soon," I added. "What time

should I bring Squib over in the morning, or will you pick him up at the Pony Club grounds?"

Katy looked surprised. "Why bother? Leave him here overnight. Help me get the ponies worked, and if you're lucky Mum will wash him while we're out, get him sparkling clean for you."

"I couldn't ask her to do that," I protested.

"You wouldn't have to ask. She loves it, honestly," Katy insisted.

To my surprise, Deb backed her up. "Go on then. I've been dying to have a go at that tail of his."

I'd thought Squib's tail was pretty clean already, but I nodded. "If you're sure. Thanks."

"No problem. Go get your ponies in Katy, and get out of my hair for a while."


When I'd seen Katy riding her stunning chestnut pony at our Pony Club rally, I'd never imagined that only two days later I'd be sitting on his back myself, but half an hour on that was exactly what I was doing. I was nervous to begin with, worried about ruining him, but Katy had laughed off my concerns.

"I wouldn't let you ride him if I didn't think you could manage. Don't worry, Lucas is idiot-proof. Not that you need him to be. You ride fine, stop panicking about it."

The blue roan pony she was riding danced sideways, almost ramming her leg into a gate post, and Katy scolded her mildly.

"Excuse me, Fossick? What kind of behaviour do you call that? Have some manners, honestly." She grinned at me. "Just be glad I'm not making you ride this nutter."

"She's really cute. I love her tail."

The mottled black and white pony had a mostly white tail with a wide black streak at the top, making her look somewhat like a skunk.

"I know. I wanted to call her Flower, like the skunk in that cartoon, but Mum vetoed it."

"Fair call," I replied. "Flower's kind of a dumb name for a pony."

"Whatever, it's cute. Better than Fossick. Makes her sound like some old skeleton in the ground."

"That's a fossil."

"I know. I'm not retarded." She gave me a strange look as soon as she said that, and changed the subject swiftly. "So is your other brother as hot as Anders?"

"No."

"Aha!" Katy gave a triumphant cry that spooked Fossick into tripping over her own feet, and just about face-planting into the ground. Once she'd recovered her balance, Katy turned to look at me again. "So you do admit that he's hot."

"Can we talk about ponies again?"

"Fine. What d'you think of Lucas?"

"He's wonderful."

I wasn't lying. Lucas was smooth and easy to ride, attentive to my aids and very obliging. He was like a dream of a pony, and I knew I'd never sat on anything this well-schooled before.

"Pretty cool, huh? You should give him a jump. Come on, we'll go up into the pines where I set up some cross-country jumps over winter. Don't tell Mum though, she doesn't know about them." Katy grinned at me. "Doesn't like me jumping without supervision, but it gets boring when she's always standing there telling me what I did wrong. This way!"

The ponies were puffing when we were done, and Katy looked at Fossick's sweaty neck a little guiltily as we rode back to the yard, where we could see her mum diligently washing Squib's tail.

"Wait for me to get my head torn off when Mum sees how hot Fossick is. *She's competing tomorrow, and didn't need to be worked that hard,*" she said, mimicking her mother's voice.

Sure enough, moments later Katy was getting an earful. She gave back as good as she got though, telling her mother that the pony was too fit for its own good anyway, and maybe this way she'd behave at the show instead of running through all the jumps like she had last time.

I untacked Lucas as they bickered, then went over to stare at Squib's blindingly white tail as Deb toweled it dry.

"How did you do that?"

Deb pointed to a collection of bottles sitting on the ledge next to Squib, who was standing on the concrete pad of the hosing bay. I picked the first one up and looked at it, then back at her.

"Dishwashing liquid?"

"Powerful de-greaser," Deb said. "One wash with that, rinse it out, then wash with Hi Tone Silver, rinse it out, and go again if necessary. There are a few other tricks, but this seems to have done the job."

"Wow." I watched as she sprayed Squib's gleaming tail liberally with conditioning spray, then bundled it into a tailbag. "I'll have to remember that for next time."

"Now for his socks," Deb said, and Katy let out an exasperated sigh.

"Mum, you do remember that it's just a little Pony Club sports day thing that we're going to tomorrow, not Horse of the Year."

Deb ignored her, and turned to me. "AJ, would you like to know how to get your pony's socks whiter-than-white?"

I didn't hesitate. "Yes please."

Katy rolled her eyes, but we both ignored her, and she went to get the last pony in for riding while Deb showed me how to make a paste from talcum powder and spread it over Squib's already scrubbed white socks, then wrap them in stable wraps to keep them clean overnight.

"He can stay in tonight with Fossick," she said. "We're a bit short on grass at the moment but we'll give him plenty of hay."

"Okay," I said. "I don't know if he's ever been in overnight before though."

"He'll be fine. We'll keep a close eye on him. Or you could stay over, if you wanted to. Keep an eye yourself."

It was only then that it occurred to me that Dad had no idea where I was. I'd left him a note that morning, explaining that I was going riding with a friend, but I'd left the house before eight and it was now almost five o'clock. Even worse, I'd left my cellphone in my bedroom at home, still on its charger.

"Um, can I borrow your phone?"

"Sure. Stay for dinner too, if you like. I can run you back to your place afterwards to get what you'll need for the night, and for tomorrow. And it'll give me a chance to meet your parents, reassure them that I'm not trying to kidnap you or anything."

I followed her into the house, and picked up the phone, quickly dialing home. Dad picked up on the third ring.

"Hello?"

"Hi Dad, it's AJ."

"Oh hi Possum, how are you?"

He didn't sound worried at all, and my relief at not being in trouble was tempered by a flash of annoyance. He probably hadn't even noticed that I'd been gone all day.

"Fine. I'm over at a friend's place, and they've invited me and Squib to stay overnight and go to a show with them tomorrow." I could sense Deb hovering in the background, probably waiting to see if my parents wanted to talk to her. "They're going to drop me home after dinner to pick up my things, so you can meet them then. They're really nice," I added.

"Uh huh, that sounds fine," Dad said vaguely. "I can get your brother to bring your things to you, if that's easier. That'll save putting your friends out. Just let me know what you need."

I gritted my teeth. You'd think having a detective for a mother who spent her days investigating homicides would make your family suspicious of you hanging out with unknown people, but you would be wrong. Anything that got me out from under their hair worked for my dad.

"Um, I think it'd be better if I came and got them," I said. "It's too hard to explain what I need and the stuff is all over the place."

Dad was unfazed. "Okay, well come by anytime."

*Of course I will. I do still live there*, I wanted to remind him, but I schooled myself to patience.

"Okay. See you later." I hung up the phone and turned to Deb. "It's fine with him."

She nodded, looking pleased. "Super. I think Katy's got

Forbes in now, so if you could help her get him worked while I get dinner started, that'd be great."

"Sure." I headed quickly towards the door, grateful that I'd found somewhere that I could be useful.

# 6

## SLEEPOVER

Dax barked at us as we walked up the front steps to my house later that evening, came bounding out when I opened the door, then raised his hackles and growled low in his throat at the sight of strangers.

"Dax, be nice," I told him. "Sorry. He's an ex-police dog and he takes his job very seriously."

Katy looked slightly alarmed by the huge German Shepherd, but when I rubbed Dax's head and told him to be polite, he obediently sat down and offered a paw to shake. Katy laughed.

"You better shake it or he'll think you're being rude," I said to her, and she obliged.

Dax decided she was probably okay, and started sniffing her sweater, interested in the lingering smell of her little dog.

Mum was home for once, her head bent over masses of paperwork that she had strewn across the dining table. She barely looked up when I walked into the room, with Katy and Deb on my heels and Dax bringing up the rear.

"Hi Mum."

"Hello darling." She glanced up, then noticed our guests with a start. "Oh, hello."

She quickly stood up, shuffling her papers into a haphazard pile. Not quite fast enough for us to miss the gory photos of stab wounds, and Katy turned slightly green.

"Sorry, I'm just trying to get some work done. You must be AJ's new friends. Lovely to meet you."

She shook hands with Deb, and I quickly introduced them, then said I'd better go and get my things from my room.

"I'll help you," Katy said quickly, and followed me down the hallway towards my room.

My heart sank when I noticed that Anders's bedroom door was open. Worse, he was sitting on his bed with his guitar, plucking away at it. He couldn't really play much on the guitar, but he liked the way that it made him look when he held it, and as he constantly reminded me, the girls loved it. He'd had a handful of lessons and taught himself a few songs, and seemed content with that.

He glanced up as we walked past. "Hey Poss. Hey friend-of-Poss."

Katy skidded to a halt outside his door, and I stifled an internal groan. *Great.* She glanced at me with a grin.

"Poss?"

"It's a nickname. Ignore him."

Anders ran his fingers lightly over the guitar strings and smiled at Katy. "I don't think we've met."

He stood up, all six foot something of him, and walked to the doorway to shake her hand. I shot him a filthy look, but he pretended not to notice.

"I'm Anders."

"Katy."

"Nice to meet you, Katy."

"Come on," I told her. "My room's down here."

I started walking, but when I reached the end of the hall and looked back, Katy was still standing there chatting to Anders, who was leaning against the doorframe of his room with his arms folded, grinning at her.

I flung my bedroom door open and stomped in, making Astrid jump. She was lying on her bed reading a book, which was pretty much all she did when she wasn't eating or sleeping. Dad's theory was that the rest of us were so madly active that the sporty gene had expired by the time it came to Astrid. She unplugged a headphone from one ear and looked at me.

"Where have you been all day?"

"Riding."

"All day? Poor Squib must be exhausted."

"I was riding with my friend, on her ponies. She has six of them," I told Astrid, who raised her eyebrows.

"Wow, lucky."

"Yep."

I rummaged through my drawers, trying to find a presentable pair of jodhs to ride in tomorrow. The ones I'd worn to Pony Club on Thursday were still in the washing basket, but I had another pair that I tried to save for the most special occasions. I pulled them out and looked at them critically. Mum had picked them up second-hand almost a year ago, and they'd been a tight fit then.

"You'll never get back into those," Astrid said helpfully.

"Shut up."

She rolled onto her stomach again, and I stuffed the jodhs

into my bag anyway, hoping for the best. My show jacket was in the wardrobe, and it would definitely still fit, since it had been three sizes too big when I got it. I had been meaning to get it dry-cleaned, because it still had a trail of Squib's snot across one shoulder from the last time I'd worn it, but I'd expected to have more than a few hours warning before the next show I attended. I shoved it into my bag with a shrug, reassuring myself that at least Squib would look good tomorrow. Hopefully his blindingly white tail and socks would distract from his scruffy rider.

Katy appeared in the doorway just as I zipped my bag shut. "Is this your room?"

"Yeah." I motioned towards my sister. "That's Astrid. This is Katy."

Astrid rolled over again and looked at Katy with interest.

"Are you the one with six ponies?"

I felt my face flush, but Katy just nodded as she came further into the room.

"That's me."

"You must be rich."

Katy shrugged. "Not really. Mum's a hoarder."

She looked at the handful of ribbons pinned to the wall above my bed, and my embarrassment increased as I mentally compared the meagre offering to the masses of winnings that decorated her house.

"Okay, let's get out of here."

"All right. Nice to meet you Astrid," Katy said with a smile, but my little sister had already stuck her headphones back in and returned to her book.

Anders was still strumming away on his guitar when we passed his room.

"See ya," I called on my way past, and he slapped his hand over the strings, stopping the reverberation of sound.

"Good luck at your horse thing," he yelled back. "Kick some ass, take some names."

Katy was right behind me as we approached the kitchen. "He's so nice."

"Yeah, sure."

Mum and Deb were getting on famously, sitting at the table chatting non-stop.

"That was quick," Deb exclaimed as we came back into the room. "It always takes Katy half an hour to get ready for anything."

"It does not. Stop exaggerating."

Mum and Deb gave each other commiserating looks, presumably about the rudeness of teenage girls, before Deb stood up.

"Well, I suppose we'll be off and let you get back to work."

"Lovely to meet you," Mum said, and I shifted my weight restlessly while I waited for them to finish making pleasantries. There was something about having Katy and Deb in my house that was making me uneasy, and if Anders decided to make another appearance, Katy was likely to melt into a puddle and have to be siphoned off the floor. But finally we made it outside, and as we walked back to Deb's car, I felt like I could breathe again.

"They seem lovely," Deb said.

"Yeah," I muttered noncommittally.

She started the engine and backed out across the gravel as I stared at the bag in my lap and wondered how ridiculous I was going to look tomorrow in my shabby second-hand clothes. I hoped I wasn't about to make a complete fool of myself.

I woke up early the next morning, and lay on the couch staring at the row of shiny trophies arranged on the mantelpiece opposite. Were Katy and her mum going to expect me to win today, when I'd never even managed to jump a clear round at a show? They were clearly competitive and used to winning, and my stomach cramped nervously. I hoped I wasn't going to let them down.

Deb was up first, and came quietly into the room to get breakfast started. I sat up quickly, and she smiled at me.

"Morning. Did I wake you?"

"I was awake." I shimmied out of the sleeping bag they'd provided me and ran my fingers through my tangled hair.

"Nervous?" Deb asked with a smile, seeming to read my mind.

"A bit," I admitted. "You've been so good to me, I don't want to let you down."

She shook her head at me. "Don't worry. If it doesn't go well, we just put it down to mileage. There's always another day."

I nodded, rummaging through my bag and pulling out my jodhs and a t-shirt. "I'll just get dressed."

"Okay. Can you bang on Katy's door when you go past, make sure she's getting up?"

Katy was still in bed with a pillow over her head. I told her to get up, but she just mumbled something unintelligible and pulled the blankets up higher.

In the bathroom, I washed my face and changed my shirt, then looked at my jodhs skeptically. Astrid had been right – they looked way too small for me. Resolutely I gave it a go, just in case, but I could barely scrape them over my thighs, and there was no way they would reach my waist, let alone fasten.

Tears sprang into my eyes as I mentally kicked myself. Why hadn't I just fished out my dirty pair and brought them? I could even have asked to wash them here, or got Mum to wash them at home last night and picked them up on the way to the show this morning, but I had stubbornly pretended that I would fit into my outgrown jodhs, and now I was going to have to go into the kitchen and admit to Deb that I had nothing to wear.

Katy's room was empty when I passed it, and my heart sank to see her sitting at the kitchen counter with a plate of toast, still in her pyjamas but very much awake. Her eyes scanned me, taking stock of my pyjama shorts and the jodhs I was carrying in one hand.

"All good?"

I shook my head, and to my horror I could feel the tears threatening behind my eyes again. *Pull yourself together, AJ!* I took a breath, and confessed.

"I'm so dumb. I packed the wrong pair of jodhs, and these ones don't fit me anymore. Do you think we could go past my place on the way to the show and pick up another pair?"

They'd be filthy, but dirty was better than non-existent.

Deb frowned. "We could, but it's a bit out of the way. Why don't you borrow a pair from Katy?" She looked at her daughter. "Go find AJ something that'll fit her."

Katy shoved the rest of her toast into her mouth and jumped

down from the bar stool. "C'mon then."

Ten minutes later, I stood in front of her bedroom mirror and stared at myself. Her cream breeches fit me like a glove, and on discovering that I didn't have a proper show shirt, Katy had insisted that I borrow one of those as well. The bright red shirt with its white collar looked amazing, and I turned side-on, unable to quite believe how professional I looked.

"Perfect. You can keep those jodhs," Katy told me, flopping back onto her bed with a satisfied sigh.

"Don't be ridiculous."

"Why not? They don't fit me anyway. I won them in a raffle, but they're too big on me and they look all saggy." She pulled a face, then sat up. "Not that you're fat. I've just got stick legs."

"Yeah, I noticed."

"At least you have boobs. Flat as a pancake, over here," she said sadly, then sat up again and went back to her closet. "Actually, try this on too. I made Mum buy it because I loved it so much, but it's too broad in the shoulders and looks stupid on me. I wore it once and then saw photos and was so disgusted that I haven't worn it again, which drives Mum crazy because it was *not* cheap."

She pulled a show jacket off its hanger and held it out to me, and I took it. It was black with silver lining, and a subtle grey trim on the collar and pockets. It was far nicer than my jacket, which was going to look utterly ridiculous with the rest of Katy's clothes, but I felt a bit self-conscious as I pulled it on.

"I feel like a dress-up doll."

Katy laughed. "You're my very own life-size Barbie. That's perfect! Ugh. It looks so much better on you than it does on me. Oh well, at least it'll be getting some use. Now, let's get breakfast finished before we load the ponies."

Back at the breakfast bar, Katy started filling out my late entry form for the day. My appetite had returned momentarily, although now that both Squib and I were going to look the part, I was getting even more nervous about letting the side down.

"What's Squib's show name? Does he have one?"

I blushed. "Yeah, it's Squirrel Nutkin."

Katy looked up with a grin. "Seriously?"

"I know, it's stupid."

"No it's not! It's the cutest thing ever. *Squirrel Nutkin*," she repeated, writing it on the entry form. "That's awesome. And it totally suits him. He is a bit of a nut. Besides, it's better than having a pony named after a sports drink."

"Huh?"

"HK Lucozade. It's Lucas's show name, and I hate it."

"Why don't you change it?" I suggested, but Katy shook her head.

"Can't. It's his stud name, he's always been registered with that name, and he's got a competition record as long as my arm. Be crazy to change it now. Besides, he doesn't belong to me, so I couldn't even if I wanted to."

"Really? Whose is he?"

"He still belongs to Abby Brooks. She produced him when she was on ponies, and never wanted to sell him. When I got Molly on lease from Steph, Abby liked how she went for me so she gave me Lucas to ride as well. When I move off ponies, he'll go on lease to someone else. Which will be the worst day of my life, probably."

"You don't own Molly either?"

"Nope. I've got a paddock full of borrowed ponies out there. Robin and Foss and the Forbester are the only ones that are technically mine."

Something clicked in my head then, as I realised why Katy was so keen to make money from selling her other ponies. I'd assumed she would be able to sell Lucas and Molly when she was done with them, and that they'd make her enough money to buy two Young Rider horses if she wanted to, but it turned out that wasn't the case at all.

# 7
# SHOWTIME

When we arrived at the show grounds, Squib was so excited to be somewhere new that he literally launched himself off the truck ramp, tearing the rope from my hands. Fortunately when he landed he was so overcome that he stopped to look around, and Katy quickly grabbed him, laughing at his antics. I hurried down the ramp behind him, nursing my rope-burned hand, and tied him to the side of the truck, where he spun around and whinnied loudly.

To make matters worse, we'd parked only a few vehicles down the row from Donna, who was standing behind her float with her hands on her hips, glaring across at Squib. She took two steps towards me, and I hurried back up the ramp to help Katy unload the rest of the ponies. By the time I was leading Fossick down the ramp, Donna had disappeared again, and I breathed a sigh of relief.

Deb was amazing. Whenever I'd been to a show before, I'd had to try and organise myself, and I never really knew what I was doing. As a result, I'd been eliminated before I'd even started more than once, and was usually either stupidly early or really late for my classes. But Deb had a whiteboard on the wall of the truck that she wrote the names of all the ponies on, with their class numbers and approximate start times. She'd gone over to the office first thing to put my late entry in, and when I was ready to ride, she led Squib up to me with his mane and tail as white as snow, his hooves painted black and his socks so blindingly clean that I could hardly stand to look at them. I almost couldn't believe that this was my pony. With his borrowed martingale, jumping boots and bright white saddle blanket, which Deb had shoved at me and insisted I used, the only thing letting the side down was the shabby Wintec saddle. And once I was sitting in it, nobody would even notice that.

"He looks amazing," I gasped as Deb gave me a leg-up onto his back.

"He'll look even better when he gets some proper muscle," Katy told me as she tightened Fossick's girth. "Once we get rid of that ugly bulge on the underside of his neck and get some real power over his hindquarters, he'll be a completely different shape. And then you'll *really* have a show jumping powerhouse."

"I'm not sure I need any more power than I already have," I replied as we rode towards the ring, side by side. "It's hard enough keeping up with him as it is."

"That's just because he's green, mostly. And he gets so overexcited about jumping. Once he gets more used to it, he'll settle down and become more rideable. Besides, what a problem to have – your pony's too talented. Poor you!"

Deb held the ponies while we walked the course for the first class. Katy had scoffed and insisted she didn't need to walk such a baby course, but Deb had told her to go with me, so she'd reluctantly complied.

"That's the first jump there," I said, pointing towards the yellow and white oxer with the jump number 1 next to it. "Then the blue and white."

I started strolling towards the second jump, but Katy pulled me up.

"Where are you going?"

"To the second jump."

"You haven't walked the first one."

I looked at her, confused. "I know where it is – right there."

A slow smile crept over Katy's face. "Yeah, but you have to actually walk to it. Haven't you done a course walk before?"

"Um…"

"Okay. First we find the start flags. Which are about three strides away from the first fence, so that's easy."

Katy walked towards the yellow oxer, and I hurried to catch up. She strode purposefully towards the jump, walking right up to the middle of the pole and then turning her head towards the second fence.

"Look for your second jump from here."

Katy raised an arm to point towards it, then walked around the other side of the jump and stood with her back up against the back rail. She took one long stride, then four normal steps, counting as she went.

"*One* two three four. *Two* two three four. *Three* two three four."

I copied her as we walked the slightly bending line towards fence two. "Six strides, nice and easy. Now, where's fence three?"

I followed Katy around the course, learning more than I'd ever realised I didn't know. As we walked back through the finish flags, Katy stopped and reviewed the whole course.

"One - the yellow oxer, six bending strides to two, the blue vertical. Go left around the wall to the green oxer, five strides to the planks, then it's a right turn to the two-stride double, and that's short and starts with an oxer so make sure you sit up and hold him…"

I'd never felt so prepared in my life as I did when I rode into the ring for that round. Deb had helped me warm up over the practice jump, starting with a cross bar and building it up to a vertical, then moving on to the oxer. Jumping and making a smooth turn in either direction, halting Squib when he got too strong.

"Don't be afraid to do that in the ring," she advised me. "I mean, not right in front of a jump or you'll confuse your pony, but if you need to stop or circle, do it. If he's on the wrong leg, bring him back to trot and fix it, don't let him skid around the corner on the wrong lead or he won't be balanced enough to make a good jump. This is a schooling round, and we just want him to go around steadily and under control."

It wasn't easy, and Squib got a bit strong, but I only had to circle him twice. Once was coming towards the double, when he saw it and accelerated, but after I made him trot a circle and then cantered back towards the combination, he jumped through neatly. Although every time we circled it counted as a refusal, we didn't knock any fences down, and I came out of the ring feeling like we'd made a real go of it.

Deb congratulated me on my good riding, and Katy high-fived me on her way into the ring on Fossick. I walked Squib back and forth along the edge of the ring, watching Katy ride.

Fossick was excited too, but much more controlled than Squib, and Katy jumped an easy clear round. She didn't get to rest on her laurels for long though, because as soon as she was out of the ring on Fossick she was swapping onto Forbes, and warming him up. I took Squib back to the truck and unsaddled him and left him with a haynet before going back to watch Katy ride again.

She got both ponies into the jump off, and I was holding Forbes while she got Fossick ready when Donna walked up to me.

"I see you've made friends in high places."

I looked over at her. "Yeah, they've been really helpful."

She scanned me from head to foot, and I knew she was taking note of the fact I was wearing someone else's clothes.

"I see they finally got you to put a martingale on that pony of yours. I have been telling you that for months, you know."

*Yelling at me to 'tie that damn pony's head down and get it under control' isn't quite the same as explaining why I should use a piece of tack and letting me experiment with it*, I wanted to tell her, but I bit my tongue. Donna had a lot of influence in the Pony Club, and I needed the grazing that they supplied. It was the cheapest around by a long shot, and I couldn't afford to make her mad, as much as I wanted to give her a piece of my mind.

Then Deb came over, and Donna turned into sweetness and light, thanking her for taking me under her wing, and saying how marvellous it is to have her helping out at grass roots level.

"I wouldn't call AJ 'grass roots'," Deb said calmly. "She's a very competent rider, and has been a great help to Katy, getting all her ponies worked this weekend. She's got the makings of a super groom too, now that she's learning the tricks of the trade."

I flushed with pride under her praise, and watched Donna quickly backtrack and agree that I was doing very well with a difficult pony and (in hushed breath) *'limited family support'*.

"Well, we're not all lucky enough to have parents who have the time and money to invest in the sport," Deb replied as I flushed an angry red. "My parents didn't know the first thing about horses, so I learned it all the hard way and just absorbed information like a sponge from everyone I met. Katy's had it a bit easier, but ponies like this keep her honest," she added, motioning to Fossick bucking her way around the corner in the jump-off.

I turned to watch as Katy used all her skill to get the pony straight to the planks, but she managed it somehow and Fossick jumped cleanly over before galloping to the last and clearing it easily to notch up the winning time.

"First again," Katy said with satisfaction later that morning as she rode back to the truck on Robin, her feet dangling from the placid pony's stirrups. "Not that there's much competition out there. Robin could jump that course with his eyes closed."

"Behave yourself," her mother scolded as Katy jumped to the ground and pulled the red ribbon off Robin's neck.

It fluttered to the ground at the foot of the ramp, and I reached down and picked it up, running the red satin through my fingers. I'd never won first place at a show in my life, but Katy seemed completely unmoved by her success. She tied Robin to the truck and loosened his girth, then ran up his stirrups and removed his bridle.

"Right, Mr Plod. You can stand here and go to sleep for a

while until the Championship starts. Who's on next?"

"Forbes in the metre," Deb told her. "Squib too. But you've got time for a sandwich first, if you want one."

"Yeah, okay." Katy climbed the ramp into the truck and walked through into the accommodation, flopping down on the sofa and stretching her long legs out in front of her. "Ham and cheese, and some of that pickle spread if we've got any left."

"I think you ate it all at Hawera last weekend," Deb told her as she took a loaf of bread out of the cupboard.

Katy pulled a face at her. "You should've said, we could've restocked."

"Oh well, you'll live. AJ, are you hungry?"


The course for the metre class wasn't as straight-forward as the ninety, and had a one-stride double, which I'd never attempted before on Squib.

"Take a hold coming into it, you'll be fine," Katy assured me. "Just don't let him run at it, or he'll probably try and take it as a spread! Just sit up, lots of half-halting on the way to it, then let him do his job."

It sounded easy, but it wasn't. The rest of the course had disappeared behind us with relative ease, and I hadn't even had to circle him yet, but when we came to the double Squib took hold and tried to rush towards it. I did my best to steady him up, but he fought against me, and it was suddenly too late to turn away and circle. I let him go, hoping for the best. He flung himself into the air over the first, jumping it much bigger than he needed to, and landed way out. I put my leg on and he took one stride, but we ended up much closer to the second fence than we'd planned. Squib baulked in astonishment, and I thought he was going to refuse. *Good job, AJ, now you've made your brave pony have a refusal.* Squib had never in his life stopped before, and my heart sank.

But Squib wasn't going down without a fight. He sank back onto his hindquarters, then launched himself into the air, trying to clear the jump. Unfortunately, he had enough height but not enough width, and he landed in the middle of the wide oxer. The poles crashed down around us and Squib stumbled, pitching me forward onto his neck. I lost a stirrup and clung tight as he scrambled through the falling poles, eventually regaining his balance. I was still swinging around his neck, and totally fed up with my inept riding, he threw a huge buck and sent me flying onto the ground.

Katy's head appeared in the doorway of the ambulance, and she looked at me in concern.

"You okay?"

I nodded as the paramedic strapped my aching wrist. "Just a sprain."

"No more riding today though," the medic insisted, and Deb nodded.

"I think we're done for the day. Never mind," she said, patting me on the shoulder sympathetically, and I tried not to wince, knowing I would have a decent bruise there by tonight.

"Is Squib okay?" I asked Katy.

"Yeah, he's fine. Stuffing himself with hay, none the worse for wear."

"I feel terrible," I confessed to her as we walked back towards the truck, finally dismissed by the paramedic. "It was my fault that we crashed."

"Not really," she shrugged. "You tried to tell him to slow down, but he wasn't listening. Probably should've circled though."

"Yeah."

"I thought for a second he was going to jump it as a bounce," Katy grinned. "That would've been epic."

"It just sucks that he's ending the day with a bad experience," I told her as we came in view of my pony, happily munching on hay at the side of their truck. My heart swelled at the sight of him, despite the pain in my arm. It wasn't his fault that I hadn't set him up properly.

"I'll ride him if you want," Katy offered suddenly.

"Really? You'd want to?"

"Are you kidding? I'd *love* to. I've been dying for a sit on him since I first saw him jump."

I grinned at her, overwhelmed by her generosity. "That'd be great! I'm sure he'd love that too."


Later that afternoon, I stood with my arm in a sling and watched as Squib trotted into the ring for the metre-five speed class.

"Last to go will be Katy O'Reilly riding Squirrel Nutkin," the announcer said, and rang the bell to start.

Katy sat down in the saddle and Squib leapt into his bounding canter. I'd never seen him being ridden by anyone else before, except when we'd first gone to look at him before he was mine, and I was overcome with pride as my gorgeous pony cantered through the start flags and leapt over the first jump, clearing it with masses of air.

I laughed. "He jumped that one huge!"

Deb looked at me with a smile. "He always does that."

"Does he really?"

I knew that he jumped high, but I'd never realised until now just how much energy and power Squib put into jumping. He was even more impressive from the ground than he felt from the saddle, and I grinned proudly as Katy rode a clear round. She even made it neatly through the one-stride double, carefully holding him back from the turn so that his stride was shorter and more contained all the way to the jumps. He jumped neatly over the first, took one stride, then she let him go and he exploded over the second, clearing it by miles.

I laughed again. "He's so ridiculous."

"He's amazing," Deb said. "You've got yourself one hell of a pony right there."

Even though Katy hadn't been riding for time, there weren't many entries in the class, and Squib was the only one who jumped a clear round, so he ended up winning. I couldn't believe it as I watched Katy canter the lap of the ring, laughing at Squib as he tried to get his head down so he could buck. The red ribbon looked glorious against his dark grey coat, but as proud as I was of my pony's efforts, I couldn't help feeling a bit jealous. Katy won so effortlessly – she'd literally won every class she'd entered today, including a purple sash for taking out the Show Hunter Championship on Robin – and she didn't even seem to care.

That afternoon as the ponies were being prepared for the trip home, Katy was in the truck counting up the prize money.

"Eighty-five bucks," she declared. "Not bad for entries that cost less than half that. Oh, here."

She handed me a small brown envelope, and I looked at it in confusion. *1.05m Pony 1st* was scrawled on the front in blue ballpoint, and I realised that it was Squib's winnings.

"I can't take that."

"You paid the entry."

"Yeah, but you won the class. Plus you brought me here and had Squib overnight, and he's already eaten his weight in hay since he got to your place yesterday." I shoved the envelope back at her. "Seriously. Keep it."

Katy shrugged. "Okay. A hundred and five bucks. Even better."

I reached into my pocket then, and pulled out the red ribbon I'd removed from Squib's neck. "Oh, and here. You should have this too."

Katy looked at it in surprise. "I don't want it."

"But you won it." I laid it on top of the pile of red ribbons sitting in the truck.

"I'm about to take all these back to the office," Katy told me. "Ribbons are expensive, and when we come to little shows like this we often donate them back to the club. Especially ones like this," she added, tugging at the tasselled end of the purple sash Robin had won. "They'll only end up in a box under my bed otherwise." She grabbed up the ribbons in her fist and started down the ramp, and I spoke before I could stop myself.

"In that case, give us Squib's one back. It's the first time he ever won anything, I might as well keep it for posterity."

Katy held the fistful out to me, and I grabbed one of the red ribbons and pulled it free from her hand. I had no idea if it was the one he'd actually won, but it was good enough. I shoved it back into my pocket, the whole situation feeling weirdly anticlimactic.

# 8

# RED RIBBON

It was getting dark when I got home that night. Deb had dropped Squib off at the Pony Club paddock on the way back from the show, and had insisted that I continue borrowing the bit and martingale until I either bought my own or didn't need them anymore. Katy had made me promise to come over and ride with her during the week, before they headed off to a four-day show over the weekend. They'd invited me to go with them, but I knew there was no way I'd be allowed the time off school, so I'd regretfully declined.

"Oh well. Once we're back, school will be out for two weeks and we can ride together every day," Katy had said.

"Steady on," Deb had cautioned her daughter. "AJ might have plans with her friends, or a family trip away."

I shook my head. "We don't really get away much. And I think I have a party to go to, but I don't have much planned really. I'd love to come and ride with you," I'd told Katy, and she'd given her mother a smug look.

Squib had galloped off across his paddock in delight when I let him go, making Katy laugh with his bucking and farting as he went to look for his friends. She'd helped me put my gear

81

away in the shed, then they dropped me off at the bottom of my driveway. I jumped down from the cab and dragged my bag out of the accommodation.

"Thanks so much, for everything," I said, but they waved off my gratitude.

"Anytime," Deb assured me. "It's been lovely having you."

"Don't be a stranger. I want to see you later this week!" Katy yelled out of the window as they drove away and I walked up to my house, the world coming back to normal around me at last.

The whole weekend seemed like a dream, except that it had really happened, and I still had the red ribbon in my pocket to prove it. It would've been nicer to have won it myself, but it was still Squib who'd earned it, even if I hadn't. It was still important.

I let myself in the front door and found Alexia sitting on the couch with her head buried in a book of Sudoku puzzles. I didn't even know where to start with those things, but Lexi could spend hours doing them without getting bored. She didn't look up when I came into the room, and I would've escaped unnoticed down the hall except that Anders came out of the kitchen and spotted me.

"She's alive! Well, barely. What've you done to your arm?"

He was staring at my sling, and I shrugged. "Fell off."

Anders shook his head, a mocking smile on his face. "I don't believe that was in the game plan."

"Yeah, well. Things don't always go according to the game plan. But check this out," I said, whipping the red ribbon out of my pocket and waving it in his face.

"Can you stop talking please!" Alexia snapped, only adding

*please* to the end of the sentence as part of its syntax, not because she was trying to be polite. "I'm trying to concentrate on this puzzle." She looked up at us accusingly, then her eyes caught the thin strip of red satin in my hands. "What's that? Let me see."

Her hand shot out and made a grab at Squib's ribbon. For a fraction of a second as her fingers closed around it I hesitated, wanting to pull it away and tell her she couldn't have it. I was tired of her having everything she wanted. But she was already pulling it through my fingers, and I let it go, knowing that if I didn't there'd be hell to pay.

Alexia ran the ribbon through her fingers, her mouth moving as she silently read the words printed in silver across the bright red fabric. *WOODVILLE PONY CLUB – 1ST PLACE.* Her fingertips traced the horseshoes at either end of the words reverently, putting every ounce of focus she had into the sensation of touch. I knew that my ribbon was lost into her hands, at least for a while. I wanted to take it to my room and pin it over my bed, but I was pretty sure she wouldn't be giving it up without a fight.

"All right Lex, give it back now," Anders said, going into bat for me.

Alexia's fingers closed around the fabric, scrunching it slightly, and I put my hand on Anders's arm.

"Don't worry. Let her have it."

"I think I want to keep it," Alexia said firmly.

"You can't keep it, AJ won it," Anders countered. "It's hers, but you can look at it."

Alexia's face crumpled, and I jumped in quickly. "I didn't

83

win it, actually. She can have it. I don't care."

I picked my bag up and walked out of the room, leaving Alexia cradling the ribbon, but Anders followed me.

"You don't have to let her get away with that."

"It doesn't matter."

"Of course it does."

I said nothing, just walked into my room and dumped my bag on the bed. Astrid was in her usual spot, curled up in the corner with her back against the wall and a book in her hands. She glanced up as we came into the room, then frowned and turned the volume up on her iPod as Anders kept arguing with me.

"You can't just let her take whatever she wants off you. She has to learn that she can't get away with that kind of stuff."

"Leave me alone, Anders."

He wasn't giving up. He leaned his shoulder against the wall and folded his arms stubbornly. "What did you mean, you didn't win it?"

"I didn't. I fell off, remember?" I motioned to my arm. "Katy rode him. *She* won the ribbon. So it doesn't matter. Lexi can have it if she wants. I don't care."

Anders didn't move, so I lay down on my bed and stared at the wall, ignoring him. Eventually he left, and I let my eyes linger on the ribbons above my head, the ones that I had actually earned. They'd all meant so much to me at the time, but now they seemed pathetic. Third in the Bending. Fourth in Barrel Race. Second in Best Rider, which had been a pity prize really since I'd fallen off twice that day, but the judge had said she was rewarding my positive attitude because I just kept getting back on. As if I'd had any choice. Third in the Handy Hunter, which would have been first except that Squib had tried to buck me off after we finished and the judge had penalised him for his exuberance.

*He jumped so well today,* I reminded myself. *He tried so hard. It wasn't his fault that it all went so pear-shaped.*

My arm throbbed, and I was debating whether to get up and find some painkillers or lie there and wallow in self-pity for a bit longer when someone knocked on the door, and pushed it open. I rolled over, expecting it to be Mum or Dad, but it was Anders again.

"What?"

He was holding a tray, and he walked into the room and held it out towards me. I pulled myself up into a sitting position and looked at it. A bacon sandwich with the crusts cut off, a glass of water and a packet of ibuprofen.

"Sorry you fell off." He set the tray down on my bed, and I picked up the water before it spilled all over my duvet.

"Thanks." I downed a couple of tablets and put the water on my bedside table. "I have fallen off before."

"Haven't had a sling before though. What'd you do, sprain it?"

"Yeah."

"Bummer."

"Happens."

"Sometimes." Anders and I have always been able to communicate in one-word sentences, and we often made a game out of it, seeing who would crack first. He always won.

I bit into the bacon sandwich and grinned at him as I tasted the mayonnaise. Anders hated it, but I'd eat mayonnaise with everything, and especially with bacon.

"Yum."

He shook his head. "Disgusting."

"Thanks."

"Welcome."

I ate the sandwich as Anders sat on my bed and pulled faces at Astrid, who ignored him for as long as possible, but eventually cracked and started making hideous faces back at him. We were all laughing by the time I was done, and I licked my greasy fingers in satisfaction.

"Napkin?"

"Nope."

I reached towards him and wiped my hands on his t-shirt. He shook his head at me, but didn't stop me.

"Classy."

"Always."

He stood up and picked up the tray. "Better?"

"Much."

Anders winked at me, then headed for the door. "Night."

I wasn't allowed to repeat the same word back to him - that was part of the rules. I quickly racked my brains for something to say. "Peace."

He snorted at my pathetic offering, then backed up against the wall to let Alexia march into the room.

"Here you go." She held the ribbon out towards me, crumpled in her hand, as Dad appeared in the doorway behind her. I opened my mouth to tell her that I didn't want it, but Anders caught my eye and shook his head. So I reached my hand out to my big sister and took the ribbon back. Her fingers let go reluctantly, and I smiled at her, but she wouldn't look me in the eye.

"Thanks," I told her.

Alexia turned and left the room without a backwards glance, and I smoothed the ribbon out across my lap. I still wasn't sure how I felt about it, but at least I had it back.

Dad smiled at me from the doorway. "Well done, Possum. Your arm okay?"

I looked up at him and made myself smile. "Fine."

He gave me a quick nod, said he'd be back to check on me in a second, and left the room. Anders winked at me as he balanced the tray on his fingertips, taking one finger away at a time until the whole thing was balancing on his index finger.

"Show-off," I told him, and he shot me a wide grin.

He pointed at me. "Loser."

"No way, that's one word when it's hyphenated," I argued, then stopped at the triumphant look on his face.

Astrid laughed. "You always fall for that."

Anders settled the tray back onto his palm and pointed at me. "Sucker."

He stepped through the door, shutting it behind him as Astrid returned to her book. I looked at the red ribbon for a moment longer before turning around and carefully pinning it to the wall above my bed with the rest of Squib's achievements.

# 9

# POA

In the first week of the holidays, Katy and I were sitting in her living room and making fun of a dumb horse movie when Deb came into the room looking troubled.

"Hon, turn that off for a sec. I need to talk to you."

Katy rolled her eyes but pressed *pause* as Deb tapped the cordless phone against her palm.

"Your grandmother's had a fall, and she's in hospital."

Katy paled. "Oh no. Is she okay?"

"She'll be fine, but she's broken her ankle and I'll need to go and look after her for a bit."

I watched Katy's face register the news. "How long for?"

"A week. Maybe two."

Katy's eyes went wide. "But what about Pukahu? It's next weekend, and it's the first Grand Prix of the season!"

Deb frowned. "I know, but I can't help that. You'll just have to skip it this year. I'll be home in time for Feilding at the end of the month."

"But…" Katy looked distraught, then her face lit up again. "What if I get a ride with the Fitzherberts? They'll be going for sure, and they might let me squash Lucas and Moll onto the truck. Or they could drive ours, Bradley has his HT license now. Please Mum!"

But Deb was shaking her head. "I'm not letting that boy drive our truck. No, Katy. It's one show, not the end of the world."

Her voice was resolute, and even Katy knew when she was beaten. She slumped back against the couch cushions and scowled at her mother.

"You could come to Wanganui with me," Deb offered, then smiled at the horrified look on Katy's face. "Or you can stay here and mind the ponies, but you're not staying on your own."

Katy grabbed my arm, squeezing it tight. "AJ will stay with me! She's very responsible."

"I was thinking more like asking Yvette to come and stay. Make sure you eat proper meals, and…"

"Oh my God, Mum," Katy interrupted. "We're not ten years old, we know how to feed ourselves. *And* the ponies, which is what you're really worried about. Don't stress. I'll forgive you for not taking me to Pukahu if you let AJ stay here."

"Well, if it's okay with her parents," Deb said, and Katy let out a sigh of relief. "And if she wants to, of course," she added as an afterthought.

They both looked at me, and I nodded. "I'd love to, and I'm sure it'll be fine. My parents are expecting me to be here most of the holidays anyway. They'll be thrilled, honest."

True to form, neither of my parents minded in the slightest. I think they were glad to have me out of the way for the week, and after a quick trip home to pack the things I'd need, they dropped me at the Pony Club paddock to tack up Squib and ride him over to Katy's.

"We're going on holiday!" I told my pony cheerfully as I tightened his girth.

I was about to mount up when I heard hoofbeats coming along the track, and Squib spun around to see who it was, almost flattening me against the fence.

"Oy!" I prodded him in the side with my knuckles, and he moved away from me, reluctantly at first, then more smoothly when I insisted. *Maybe all that rope twirling really does have its uses,* I thought to myself as I stepped around my pony to see Carrie trotting towards me on placid little Oscar, bouncing loosely in the saddle with a wide grin.

"Hi AJ!"

"Hi Oscar. How's Carrie today? Behaving herself?" I asked.

Carrie laughed. "He says yes, and he wants you to give him a carrot."

"I'm all out of carrots today, sorry mate," I apologised to the fluffy pony, giving his forehead a quick scratch as Squib strained at his halter, trying to get close enough to say hi to his friend. "Maybe Carrie will give you a big bucket of feed instead."

"Not a *big* bucket, he might get colic," Carrie told me seriously, her short legs swinging cheerfully back and forth as Oscar closed his eyes, dozing off.

Sandra was walking down the track behind her, one hand clasping Rebel's rein behind the bit as the pony tossed his head, wanting to catch up with Oscar. Alyssa was making pathetic whimpering noises and clutching the front of the saddle with one hand, and I quickly turned away and pulled down Squib's offside stirrup.

"Are you going for a ride?" Carrie asked, flopping forward onto Oscar's short neck and burying her hands in his mane. "We've just been to the river. Oscar couldn't touch the bottom, he had to *swim*!"

"That sounds fun," I said as I snapped up the chinstrap of my helmet. "I'm going to my friend's place for the week."

"For a whole week?" Carrie's mouth dropped open in astonishment. "Are you going for a sleep over?"

"I sure am. And Squib's sleeping over too," I added for the benefit of Sandra, who had just come level with us and started snapping at Carrie for leaving her sister behind and upsetting Rebel.

"Mum, AJ and Squib are going for a sleep over," Carrie said, oblivious to the scolding. "For a whole *week*!"

Sandra looked at me through narrowed eyes. "Is that right? You do know you'll still have to pay your grazing here even if the pony isn't actually on the property, don't you?"

I nodded, checking Squib's girth once more before swinging into his saddle. He surged forward, almost flattening Rebel, who jumped sideways onto Sandra's foot. As she swore at the poor pony, I realised belatedly that Squib's halter was still tied to the fence, but I decided that it was in my best interests not to turn back. I closed my legs around Squib's sides and he trotted eagerly up the track and off on our next adventure.

"Finally! I thought you would never get here," Katy cried when I rode up the driveway twenty minutes later. "Chuck Squib out in the orchard when he's untacked, he can hang out with Robin. I'd let him go in with the young ponies but Forbes will play silly buggers and I don't want either of them getting kicked."

I turned Squib out with Forbes, then helped Katy mix feeds and distribute them to the ponies. We leaned on the fence and watched Lucas eat, his pale yellow forelock luminescent as the sun set behind the hills.

"He really is the best pony ever," Katy sighed. "It's going to break my heart to have to give him back when I age out of ponies. Good thing that's not for a couple of years yet."

"Why don't you ask if you can keep him?" I suggested. "His owner might let you. You look after him really well."

Katy shook her head. "No way. She'll want him to go to someone else to compete, or she'll have him at home. She loves him too. And it's kind of better this way. If I owned him we'd have to sell him, because it'd be a total waste to have him sitting in the paddock and Mum would be screaming out for the money he'd go for, but then he might end up going to someone horrible and it would break my heart if he got ruined. At least Abby can always take him back from whoever's riding him if he starts going like crap."

I thought about that for a moment. "That puts a lot of pressure on you to keep him going well."

Katy groaned. "Don't I know it." She straightened up and we headed back to the house, leaving Lucas to finish his dinner in peace.

"Is it the same with Molly?" I asked, and Katy shook her head, then shrugged.

"Kind of. I got her on lease when I was twelve because she wouldn't jump very well for Steph, and they thought she'd never make Grand Prix. So she came to me to do Pony Club stuff on, because we couldn't afford anything decent at the time and I was getting sick of riding half-broke ponies and having Mum sell them as soon as they started going well. But Molly and I clicked from the start, and we've had heaps of success together, which is how I got Lucas too. So I've been really lucky, because we could never afford ponies as good as them. They're both really well-bred."

"Squib's not," I said as we walked past my pony's paddock. He was following Robin around and annoying him by nipping at the tail flap of his cover, but the patient bay pony was just plodding along a few steps ahead of him.

"What is he, Connemara?" Katy asked as we kicked our boots off at the front door.

"Half Connemara, half Welsh Cob."

Katy laughed. "Man, no wonder he's so naughty. Way too smart for his own good. I was thinking we should build some grids this week, one-strides and bounces and stuff, teach him how to collect for them, so that you're all set for your next show and you won't crash and burn. Sound good?"

"Sounds perfect."

"Cool. Now, what should we make for dinner?"

The week without Deb flew by. We got up early every morning and went to bed late each night, spending our days riding and schooling and looking after the ponies. Katy showed me how to trim fetlocks and pull manes and clip out a bridle path, and I taught her how to make macaroni cheese and the merits of a bacon sandwich with mayonnaise.

One day the farrier came, and we spent the whole morning listening to him tell us dirty jokes and pretending that we understood all of them. One afternoon it poured with rain while we were out riding on the farm, and we got absolutely drenched, coming in shivering and looking like drowned rats. On Wednesday we rode over to visit the people who owned Puppet, and jumped our ponies in their arena, which was heaps bigger than Katy's and was full of brightly-painted, professional fences.

Squib was improving every day, and Katy and I took turns jumping him. He loved going up into the pines and jumping the cross country logs, and one morning we built an obstacle course in the arena that included the mounting block, a wheelbarrow, a row of tyres standing on their sides, and an old kayak with a hole in the bottom, balanced on two sawhorses. Squib jumped everything without hesitation, as did Lucas and Molly, but Katy's other ponies weren't quite so brave.

"Come on Fossick," Katy urged the roan pony as she pointed her towards the kayak. "This is not an optional exercise. Participation is compulsory!"

Fossick approached the jump sideways, then grabbed the bit and flung herself into the air, clearing the kayak by miles. She bucked on landing, and Katy laughed as she pulled the pony's head up.

"We should get this course on video for her Trade Me ad. Make her look bold as brass, jumping all these mental things. Can you go up to the house and get the video camera?"

Ten minutes later, I filmed Fossick jumping around the entire course, although she had a couple of refusals and still jumped the kayak like a lunatic, no matter what Katy did to dissuade her.

"We'll just edit out all the bad parts," Katy told me cheerfully. "Nobody ever has to know that she doesn't like jumping boats, or that she throws her head up in canter transitions, or bucks if you kick her. Look."

She kicked her heels against Fossick's round sides, and the pony pinned her ears and bucked angrily, making Katy laugh. "She's so funny."

"They might notice those things when they come and ride her," I pointed out, but Katy shrugged.

"We'll just hope we get lucky and someone wants her sight unseen. It does happen sometimes. If not, oh well. Maybe she'll be having a good day."

"It's not very honest though, is it?" I asked later that evening as Katy composed a sale ad for Fossick.

She'd edited the footage I'd taken together seamlessly, and I had to admit that based on the video and the photos that she'd selected, Fossick looked like a bold, promising young jumping pony.

"What's dishonest about that?" Katy demanded, turning her laptop screen towards me.

I scanned the text of the ad, trying to find something in there that wasn't true. There wasn't anything, really. Fossick *was* a clever, smart jumper with good technique, she *was* easy to handle and straight-forward to ride, and showed promise for show jumping or eventing. I searched the words for an outright lie, but there wasn't one. *And yet…*

"It just doesn't sound like Fossick."

Katy raised her eyebrows. "What would you have written?" I shrugged, and she opened a blank document and shoved the laptop towards me. "You write her ad then."

"I don't know her well enough," I hedged, sensing that I'd offended my friend.

"Write one for Squib. Pretend you were going to sell him." Katy got up and went to the pantry to get some biscuits. "I'm making Milo, do you want one?"

"Sure." I looked at the blank screen for a moment, then started typing.

*14.2hh Connemara x Welsh Cob gelding, 6 years old.*

That was the easy part. I muddled through the rest, being as honest as I could. Katy came back and read over my shoulder as the hot drinks heated in the microwave, and when I was done she shook her head at me.

"That is the worst *For Sale* ad I've ever read in my life."

"What's wrong with it?"

"Look at all these negative words. *Strong. Wilful. Needs experienced rider.*"

"It's true."

"Yeah, but you don't need to say it like that."

"What would you put?"

Katy cracked her knuckles and sat down next to me, pulling the laptop back towards her and deleting everything I'd written after the first sentence.

*Amazing Grand Prix prospect with talent to burn*, she typed. *Huge scopey jump, exceptionally brave and honest. Winning easily at 1.05m with very limited outings, will go all the way to the top with the right rider. Fantastic to work with, 100% sound, straight and clean legs.*

She sat back in satisfaction as I stared at the ad. "That's really what you'd write?"

"Yep. Then I'd put POA at the bottom and let them fight it out."

"POA?"

"Price on application. Then they have no idea whether you want five or fifteen thousand, but when they ring up and ask about it, you just say that you've got heaps of interest in him and you're actually thinking of maybe keeping him a bit longer because he'll be worth heaps more in a few weeks with more mileage under his belt, and they start falling all over themselves to make you an offer, and the next thing you know you've got twenty-five grand in the bank for a pony that's only ever been to a handful of shows in his life."

I stared at her. "Wow. Is that really how it works?"

"Sometimes. Not always. Sometimes you get the ponies that you just can't get rid of, like this ugly little chestnut thing I had last season which we basically gave away in the end because we were so sick of him. Or the ones that everyone wants but every time you get them ready to sell they injure themselves again, and every time you take them out it's like Russian roulette whether or not you'll have a sound pony at the end of the day. We had one like that. Managed to sell her eventually, after about six or seven stupid injuries that cost us loads in vet bills, and we let her go for a song because we just wanted rid of her while she was still sound. Of course she's never been lame a day in her life with her new owners," Katy lamented. "Typical."

She got up to fetch our mugs of Milo as I scanned over the ad she'd written for Squib again.

"Do you really think Squib would sell for twenty five thousand dollars?"

Katy laughed. "Only if you were really lucky. Probably closer to eight in his current state, but give him a season and people will be lining up to pay you the big bucks for a pony like him. He could be a real money spinner for you," she said cheerfully as she sat down on the couch and kicked her feet up onto the coffee table. "Now, what movie should we watch tonight?"

# 10
## ROUND TWO

When we arrived at Feilding two weeks later, Squib once again announced his arrival to everyone with a loud whinny as soon as we dropped the ramp.

"Shut up," I told him as I untied him. "You're such an embarrassment."

"He's just happy to be out," Katy grinned, standing at the bottom of the ramp with her arms outstretched. "Okay, I'm ready. I hope he packed his parachute!"

Fortunately this time Squib remembered his manners, and although he ran down the truck ramp, I managed to keep hold of him and got him tied to the side of the truck without mishap.

"Hi Katy!"

We both turned as a girl with a long mane of curly blond hair leapt out of the huge silver truck parked next to us and greeted Katy with a toothy smile.

"Hi Hayley!" Katy said. "How's life in the big leagues?"

Hayley pulled a face. "Not nearly so much fun."

"I bet." Katy glanced at me and clarified. "Hayley aged out of ponies last season, so she's moved on to hacks. But luckily for her, she's got a little sister who's taken over the ride on her pony."

"I wouldn't call it lucky," Hayley said testily. "Tess has had all winter to get used to Misty, but she still freaks out about jumping anything over a metre ten on him, and has flat out refused to do the Grand Prix on him today. The most I could talk her into was the Mini Prix, and she'll probably fall off at the first jump. What a waste."

I listened to them chat as I tied Forbes next to Squib. There was a girl sitting in the doorway of Hayley's truck next to us with the same curly hair and wide eyes, and I smiled at her, thinking this must be her sister Tess. She gave me a tentative smile in response.

"Who's the new pony?" Hayley asked then, standing back and admiring Squib. "He's cute."

"That's AJ's pony," Katy said, waving a hand towards me by way of introduction. "Wait 'til you see him jump. He'll be giving your Misty a run for his money in no time at all!"

Squib's first class was another ninety centimetre round, which looked significantly smaller than the same height had only two weeks ago. I walked the course on my own because Katy was jumping Forbes in the indoor, but Deb helped me get Squib warmed up. The copper roller and martingale had made a big difference, and so had the schooling that I'd given him under Katy's guidance. Deb had hardly seen Squib go since our last show, and she was blown away by his progress.

"You'd hardly know he's the same pony, except that he still clears the jumps by miles," she beamed as I stood at the gate, waiting for my turn to go in. "If he keeps improving at this rate, he'll be jumping metre-twenties by the end of the season."

The pony ahead of me finished its round with eight faults,

and I trotted Squib into the ring.

"Next to jump, AJ Maclean and Squirrel Nutkin."

There was a scattered giggle from the spectators at the announcement of my pony's name, and I flushed. I'd never liked it, but I hadn't been able to think of anything better, and as Katy said, it did suit him. Squib bounded into canter, spooking at the jumps as we cantered past them, pretending he'd never seen a coloured pole in his life before, and I had my hands full keeping him contained. He flew towards jump one and catapulted himself into the air, ears fixed forward as he kicked his heels up behind him. I dug my knees into the saddle and gathered him up for the second jump, which he cleared with equal enthusiasm.

By the time we were cantering through the finish flags, I was exhausted but exhilarated. I saw Deb standing halfway along the side of the ring, video camera in her hand as she recorded Squib's success. Katy was right behind her, sitting in Forbes's saddle and giving me a thumbs-up. I clapped my pony's solid neck and brought him back to a trot, then rode out through the gate and over to them.

I was expecting smiles and congratulations, but they looked horrified as I approached, and Katy was shaking her head at her mother.

"You didn't tell her it was an instant jump off?"

Deb shrugged, looking guilty. "I thought I did."

I pulled Squib up next to them, confused. "What's wrong?"

"You were supposed to stay in the ring and do your jump off straight away!" Katy told me. "Only Mum forgot to explain that rule to you, so now you're eliminated."

"What?"

My heart plummeted. I should have known that. I'd done instant jump off classes before, but I hadn't even thought about it. I'd been so excited by the clear round that I'd wanted to go straight to my friends and have them congratulate me.

Katy rolled her eyes at her mother, clearly blaming her instead of me, which was a bit of a relief even if it wasn't quite fair.

"I've got to get Forbes back, he was only six away when I left. Don't worry AJ, you'll make up for it this afternoon. Besides, that was the last ninety you're ever going to do. Those jumps were far too small for Squibbles!"

I felt better after I'd watched the footage of Squib's round. Despite my stupid mistake, I couldn't believe how good he looked out there, and Katy was right about the jumps. Squib cleared all of them by miles, tucking his front legs up tight and kicking his heels skyward over each fence. His blindingly white tail flew up like a pennant behind him every time he jumped, and the expression on his face was the cutest thing ever. He looked absolutely thrilled to be competing.

I watched it over and over as we ate lunch, until Hayley came in and threw herself down on the sofa next to Katy, launching immediately into a diatribe about her sister, who had apparently had a refusal in the Mini Prix that morning.

"I don't understand her. She's been handed one of the best Grand Prix ponies in the country, and she immediately turns him into a disaster! I should just give him to you to ride."

"Do it," Katy said through a mouthful of sandwich, her eyes lighting up. "I'd take him in a heartbeat."

"I wish I could. I'll try and talk Mum into it, but she keeps going on about how Tess just needs time to get used to him."

"Well he's a lot different to Rory," Katy pointed out. "Misty's not the easiest ride out, even you have to admit that."

"He's only difficult if you're scared of him. Tess just needs to harden up. Speaking of easy rides, did you see what Susannah Andrews was riding at Pukahu?"

Katy set down her plate and gave Hayley her full attention. "Oh my God. Yes. Well, I saw pictures on Facebook. I can't believe they bought him."

"I can't believe Bubbles sold him to them! Of all people… it just blew my mind when she turned up on him. Everyone's jaws were literally on the ground!"

"Poor Skybeau."

"Tell me about it."

"She wanted Forbes last season, but I was like *over my dead body*. I wouldn't sell a pony I hated to a girl like her, let alone one as lovely as Forbes."

Before I could interject to ask what was so bad about this girl Susannah, Deb came into the truck, tapping her watch.

"They've moved the Grand Prix up to one-thirty," she told Katy, who jumped to her feet. "And Lucas is second to jump, so you'd better hurry up and get ready. AJ, can you get Molly tacked for us?"

Half an hour later, I was standing at the railing in the indoor arena with Deb's video camera in my hand, preparing to film Katy's round on Lucas. The first rider was already in the ring, cantering smoothly between the fences and jumping cleanly over each one. Her pony was a gorgeous light chestnut and she rode him beautifully. I smiled as I watched, impressed by the fluidity of their round and wondering if I'd ever be able to get Squib to go like that.

The chestnut pony finished with a clear round, and a scattering of applause filled the sidelines as Katy came trotting into the ring on Lucas, his flaxen mane and tail standing out in the dim light of the indoor.

"That's all clear for Susannah Andrews and Skybeau, so they will be back for the jump off. Next to go, Katy O'Reilly on HK Lucozade."

*So that was Susannah.* As I lifted the camera to eye level, I couldn't help wondering why Katy was so adamant that she would never sell Forbes to her. I couldn't see a thing that Susannah had done wrong out there, so I could only assume that she was a horrible person who treated her ponies badly. I watched her from the corner of my eye as she rode out, but she was patting her pony kindly, and when someone at the gate congratulated her on her round, and she smiled and politely thanked them. The mystery continued. What could she have done to make Katy and Hayley hate her so much?

Lucas and Molly both jumped clear first rounds, and came back for the jump off. Molly was double clear, but Lucas had a rail at the second fence, and finished in sixth place. Molly's efforts were good enough for third, but it was Susannah who won the class, much to Katy's disgust.

"Hideously unfair," she muttered as she unsaddled Molly back at the truck.

I was crouching next to Squib, strapping on his tendon boots and trying to contain my own nerves. I'd just walked the course for my next class, and although the jumps looked tiny after the metre-thirty fences that Katy had just competed over, I was convinced that I was about to do something stupid again and ruin my own chances.

But I didn't. Squib and I jumped the best round of our collective lives, and this time I didn't leave the ring before the jump off. I brought him back to a walk after the flags, let him catch his breath, and ran my eye over the jump off course before the bell rang again. Deb had walked the course with me, telling me to just take the jump off easy and go wide on the turns, riding for a clear round instead of going fast to win, but Katy had come up to me right before I went in and told me that it was a waste of time at this height trying to do a steady double clear.

"Anyone can DC at this height, and there's forty-three ponies in your class. You can't afford to muck around out there if you want a placing. So this is what you do. Jump the first two fences like normal, make them clean, then land and turn as tight as you can, getting inside the double to the planks. Then turn tight again back to the grey oxer. Give him a straight run into the double, he's too green still to cut that corner, then let him gallop on to the triple bar. He's got the scope and the smarts to clear it from any distance. Just don't drop the reins at the base or anything dumb like that. Pretend you're on a cross country course, and just keep your eyes up and let it happen. Squib will take care of the rest."

The bell went, and I squeezed Squib back into a canter. He cleared the first two jumps easily, and when we landed I took Katy's advice, asking him to turn tightly to the left. My pony responded immediately, pivoting hard and making the turn even sharper than I'd expected him to. I lost a stirrup, but clung on and squeezed him on toward the planks. He arrived short but scraped over clean, and I got my stirrup back as I swung him back around towards the grey oxer, pushing him on strongly. Squib flew over and I sat up quickly, trying to steady him up for the one-stride double.

"Woah, pony," I said under my breath, and although he mostly ignored me, we made it through by the skin of our teeth. The back rail of the out rattled in its cups, but I ignored it and let Squib go pelting down to the triple bar. His short legs ate up the distance, his head up and his ears eagerly pricked. A wave of exhilaration washed over me as we came up slightly long, but Squib decided that the distance was manageable, and launched himself up and over with room to spare. I galloped him on through the flags, then brought him back to a steady canter, my heart pounding an excited staccato beat.

*We did it!*

"A very fast jump off for Squirrel Nutkin, clear in a time of 32.85 seconds which puts them firmly into the lead," came the announcement and I flung my arms around Squib's neck as we trotted back towards the gate.

"Nice work!" Katy reached up to give me a high five as I rode out past her. "Man, there's no stopping you two now!"

I was still buzzing half an hour later when I went in for my ribbon. One of the other competitors, a tall boy on a chunky black pony, had flown around the course and shaved two seconds off Squib's time, but finishing in second place was still a huge achievement for us and I refused to be disappointed. And as the judge tied the blue satin around my pony's neck, I was certain that this was only the start of much greater things to come.

Back at the truck, I was still buzzing as I stowed Squib's saddle away in the side compartment. I could hear Katy talking to Hayley inside the truck.

"That grey pony is awesome! He reminds me so much of Misty."

"I know," Katy agreed. "He's cool huh? He'll go Grand Prix easily."

I glowed with pride, lingering to listen to their conversation as I picked flecks of mud off the underside of Squib's stirrup irons.

"You should buy him off her. He'd be a great addition to your team," Hayley said.

I grinned, waiting for Katy to scoff at the idea, but she didn't. Instead, she said something that made my blood run cold.

"Trust me, I'm working on it."

# 11

# SQUARE ONE

I did my best to ignore Katy for the rest of the day. She had no idea why, and kept chivvying me to cheer up and talk to her, so I eventually told her that I had a migraine coming on. She became immediately sympathetic, offering me painkillers which I pretended to take, and insisting that I lie down in the back of the truck while they got the ponies sorted.

As Deb started the truck and we began rumbling out of the show grounds, Katy leaned back from the front seat and peered at me through the crawl-through.

"We'll take Squib home to ours tonight," she told me confidently. "Save you the hassle, and he's practically moved in anyway."

On any other day, I'd have been grateful for the offer, but her words sent a chill through me, and I shook my head.

"No, it's fine. He should go back to his own paddock."

Katy and Deb shared a confused look.

"Why?" Katy demanded.

"Because. I'm still paying grazing there so I might as well use it, and if I don't then they might tell me I can't come back, and I can't risk losing Squib's grazing."

Katy shrugged. "Sure you can. I was going to say you should move him to ours anyway. It's way more fun riding when you're there, and Squib loves it at our place. Plus once Fossick's sold, we'll have space for another one. Keep helping me with the ponies and we won't even charge you for grazing, right Mum?"

Deb nodded, and my heart sank. Only a couple of hours ago, I'd have been doing a happy dance at the offer, but that was the last thing I wanted now. Now that I knew Katy was trying to get her mitts on Squib. *He's my pony*, I wanted to tell her. *Not yours. Just because you're a better rider than me doesn't mean you can take my pony away.*

"No thanks," I'd said. "I'd really rather just have him go back to the Pony Club, if that's okay."

Katy started to argue again, but Deb cut her off.

"It's fine. Whatever you like. Just lie back and rest, we'll have you and Squib home in no time."

The house was quiet when I got home that night. Only Dad's car was parked outside, and I remembered belatedly that my brothers both had away games today, and Mum was probably working late again. The light was on in Dad's workshop across the lawn, and I thought of going over there to see him, but decided against it. I didn't feel much like talking right now.

My stomach rumbled, and I dropped my bags in the hallway and went through to the kitchen. Alexia was at the dining table working on a jigsaw puzzle, another one of her favourite pursuits. She was really fast at them, and they were one of the few things in the world that didn't seem to drive her mad with frustration. I pulled the fridge open and perused the contents as she methodically pieced together a wide expanse of blue sky.

"It's in the blue bowl."

I looked over my shoulder at my sister, who was still not looking at me.

"What is?"

She ignored me, but I located a blue bowl on the second shelf and looked inside. *Chicken stir-fry, yum.* Gratefully I scraped out a decent sized helping onto a plate and stuck it in the microwave. As it whirred around, I leaned my elbows on the table and watched Alexia.

"Need any help?"

She knew I was teasing, and the hint of a smile crossed the corners of her mouth. "No."

"Sure? I'm really good at jigsaw puzzles."

"No way!" she said adamantly, but she wasn't angry. She was actually in one of her better moods tonight, and I reached over and picked up a green piece and held it over the blue sky she was patching together.

"I think this one probably goes here."

"You're such an egg," she told me, but she was smiling properly now.

Every now and then I would catch glimpses of the big sister I might have had, if things had been different. I didn't blame Alexia for anything, of course, but for years it had been my biggest daydream, that she was the perfect big sister who defended me from our teasing big brothers, and who loved horses and would ride with me every day. But I'd given up on that fantasy a while ago, and after seeing the way that Hayley had treated her younger sister today, I wasn't sure I wanted

Alexia to be any other way. My perfect daydream big sister would be great, but in reality she might have been a total bitch. I looked at Alexia's long blonde hair and perfectly-formed features. Anders wasn't the best-looking person in our family, but Alexia was utterly oblivious to how beautiful she was. I wondered what she'd be like if she knew.

The microwave beeped, jolting me back to reality, and I gave my dinner a quick stir before putting it on for another minute.

"Hey Lex, check this out."

I pulled Squib's blue ribbon out of my pocket and held it out to her. Her eyes lit up for a moment, and she reached forward to take it from me, hesitating slightly as her fingers made contact.

"Can I see?"

She was really asking this time, and I nodded, realising how much of an effort it was for her to say the right thing.

"Sure."

Alexia smoothed it out across the table, reading the words carefully. "You came second."

"Yep. Out of forty-three ponies. Pretty good, right?"

She thought for a moment, then nodded. "That's *really* good."

"Thanks."

She handed the ribbon back to me as my dinner beeped again. "I liked the other one better."

"Did you?" I laid the blue ribbon on the table before turning back to the microwave. "I didn't." The second place ribbon that I earned was infinitely more important to me than the one Katy had taken for granted.

"Well you should." Alexia picked up another piece of her puzzle and examined it closely. "Red's a better colour than blue."

I chuckled. "I'll try and get more red ones in the future."

She nodded. "Good idea."

I put my bowl of stir-fry on the table and started tucking into it, reluctantly letting my thoughts flicker back across the day. I tried hard to focus on the good parts, but the memory of Katy's words lingered like a bad taste, spoiling my success. I looked at the blue ribbon disconsolately. If only we could've finished on that note. I would be on such a high right now, instead of this depressing low.

I sighed, and Alexia glanced at me, her forehead creasing into a frown. She generally struggled to read other people's emotions, but even she could tell that I was unhappy. Her hand hovered over the puzzle, still holding the pale blue piece, then she smiled and pressed it into the middle of the grass at the bottom of the landscape scene, forcing it to fit.

I knew she'd done it to try and cheer me up. I nodded at her, making a circle with my index finger and thumb and holding it up towards her.

"Perfect. Now you're getting the hang of this," I said approvingly.

Alexia looked up and met my eyes for a fraction of a second, then looked down again, a smile crossing her face as I shoved a forkload of noodles into my mouth and watched her, letting everything else fade into the background.

Nothing was the same without Katy. Our next Pony Club rally came and went, and I'd been looking forward to showing Donna how much Squib had improved. But she'd made us spend the whole rally doing flatwork without stirrups, which was still a challenge on my pony, and although I managed not to fall off, she wasn't exactly driven to shower me with praise afterwards. At least Katy hadn't been there, but then I'd known she wouldn't be. She was miles away at Te Teko, skipping school and competing all weekend.

I hadn't been able to help myself from scrolling through the results online on Sunday night, and when I'd seen that she won the Grand Prix on Lucas, I wasn't sure whether I was happy for her or annoyed that she was doing so well. I didn't know how I felt about her anymore. We'd had so much fun together, and she'd been one of the best friends I'd ever had. I had plenty of friends at school, but none of them were into horses, and they all got bored whenever I tried to tell them about Squib. Now, every time he did anything cute or funny or exceptional, I had nobody to share it with. When he jumped all the biggest jumps on our cross country course without blinking, or when he cantered a full circle on the bit without trying to pull me out of the saddle, there was nobody to high-five me and really understand what an achievement it was.

Nobody who understood, anyway. Dad would listen for hours, patiently letting my words flow in one ear and out the other, trying his best to make time for me. It wasn't the same though, knowing he didn't really get what I was talking about. Not like Katy and Deb would have. I hated that I missed them so much, but I didn't know what to do about it.

"You're friends with Katy O'Reilly, aren't you?"

I looked up from oiling Squib's bridle, the sticky rag still in my hand. Sandra stood over me as Carrie fussed around Oscar, brushing his tail with a mane comb and telling her sister that the mud on his legs was stuck there and there wasn't any point trying to get it off until it rained.

"I know her," I said noncommittally, not wanting to get into it with Sandra, who had an opinion on everyone and everything. It was none of her business anyway, but she kept prattling on.

"She has a pony for sale, and we're considering him for Alyssa. Rebel isn't working out at all. They said he was quiet when we bought him, but he's far too nervous for her and it's destroying her confidence."

*As if she has any confidence to destroy.* Alyssa would be the happiest kid in New Zealand if you told her she never had to ride again, but Sandra had committed herself to a horsy life and Alyssa's feelings no longer counted. I ran the oily rag across Squib's reins, watching the dull leather start to shine.

"Which pony?" I asked, thinking of Fossick's ad and wondering how Sandra had possibly read between the lines of that to think that she'd be in any way a suitable replacement for Rebel.

"Christopher Robin. He's a bit bigger than we wanted, full fourteen two, but she'd grow into him and they swear he's quiet as a lamb."

I thought for a moment. Robin didn't have a naughty bone in his body, and he'd be exactly the kind of pony that Alyssa needed. But despite his ponderous outlook on life, he liked getting out and doing things. He was quickly proving his talent in show hunter classes, and I knew that he would be wasted on Alyssa. And as much as I liked little Carrie, I wouldn't wish

Sandra on any pony. She never seemed to understand that ponies were animals with personalities and agendas of their own, not machines that performed exactly the same way every time you rode them.

Besides, as thrilled as Squib would be about it, the last thing I wanted was for Robin to come and graze here. What if Sandra asked Katy to come down and school him, or to give Alyssa lessons? Then she'd be turning up here, hanging around and casting her eyes over Squib, measuring him up against how well he'd be going for her if she owned him. No matter how hard I worked, without her and Deb's help, I knew I'd never measure up to his potential.

"Nah," I told Sandra. "He's not really suitable."

I was finishing my Geography assignment when Dad came into my room and sat on my bed, his hands on his knees. I knew that look. It meant he wanted to talk, and I wasn't going to be able to get rid of him until we'd had some kind of heart-to-heart. I rolled my chair back across the carpet and resigned myself to a conversation.

"What's up?"

"I was wondering how you're getting on with your pony."

*No you weren't.* "Good."

"Anything you want to talk about?"

He always started conversations this way. Giving me the chance to bring my troubles up by myself, before he did it for me. "Nope."

"Sure?"

"Yep. I need to finish this, Dad. It's due tomorrow," I told him, turning back towards my laptop, but I wasn't getting off that easy.

"What happened between you and Katy?"

I rolled my eyes. When beating around the bush failed, Dad just went straight in for the kill.

"Nothing."

"Come on, Possum. I know you're not telling me something. You two were inseparable for a while there, and suddenly you won't even talk about her."

I took a breath, collecting my thoughts. "Dad, if I told you that Squib was worth twenty five thousand dollars, would you want me to sell him?"

Dad's eyebrows shot up into his thick mop of sandy hair. "I take it this is a hypothetical scenario."

"Maybe. It doesn't matter. Just answer the question."

He thought for a moment, giving it due consideration. "Well, that would depend."

"On what?" I waited for the answer I was expecting. *On how badly we needed the money. On how well you could ride him. On what we needed for Alexia.*

"On whether or not you wanted to."

I felt tears gathering behind my eyes. I shook my head. "And if I *didn't* want to?"

"Then no, of course not. We bought you a pony to ride, not to sell."

"Even if I'm not very good at riding him, and if he'd be more successful with someone else?"

He was getting the picture now. "Did Katy tell you to sell him?"

I shook my head. "No." Giving up on my privacy, I told him

116

the whole story, and he listened thoughtfully.

"Is that all?"

"What d'you mean? Isn't that enough?"

"Did Katy ever offer you money for Squib, or try to convince you to sell him?"

I thought about those first words she'd asked me at school, before we'd become friends, and the time that she'd made me write a *For Sale* ad for my pony.

"Yes."

"Well, that's a shame." Dad stood up and squeezed my shoulder. "You two seemed to get along so well, but I'm happy to see that your loyalty lies with your pony. When we bought him for you, we hoped that you would prove that you were responsible enough to look after him, and if you've more than exceeded our expectations. I'm proud of you, AJ."

I blinked up at him. He so rarely used my name that it sounded odd coming from him.

"Thanks Dad."

"And tell Squib to keep up the good work," he added, tapping the blue ribbon on my wall that Squib had won at Feilding.

I smiled weakly at him, and once he'd left the room, I dropped my head into my hands, wondering whether I'd ever get to show jump Squib again.

# 12

# CONTRITION

It was a bit remiss of me, but it wasn't until another week had passed and a huge rainstorm was predicted that I realised I couldn't find Squib's waterproof cover. I'd searched the tack shed at the paddock and turned the garage upside down before I remembered taking it to Katy's over the holidays. I could picture it perfectly, hanging from one of the rug hooks in her neatly-organised tack room, and my heart sank. If it had been anything else, something Squib didn't really need or something that belonged to me instead of him, I'd have just left it there. But I couldn't make Squib stand out in the pouring rain over the next few days just because I was too proud to go and ask for it back.

There was only one thing for it, and no time to lose. The clouds were looming on the horizon, and a light drizzle had already started. I walked down the hall and rapped on Anders's bedroom door, then tentatively nudged it open with my toe.

"You in there?"

He was sitting on his bed surrounded by textbooks, and he looked up when I came in.

"A distraction. Exactly what I needed." His voice dripped

with sarcasm. "I'm kinda busy here, Poss."

"I need a ride to Katy's."

Anders gave me a querying look. "And?"

"And you have a car."

"Yes."

I wasn't in the mood for his games. "So will you please drive me over there?"

My brother looked strangely pleased. "I take it you two are talking to each other again at last. About time." He snapped his textbook shut and chucked it on the bed next to him as I picked at the edge of the rugby poster on his wall.

"Not exactly."

Anders narrowed his eyes at me. "So the moping is going to continue?"

"I'm not moping."

"Uh, yeah you are. You've been walking around this house like a sad sack for the last three weeks and it's driving us all up the wall. I figured you two'd had some kind of teenage girl falling out, but I thought it would've blown over by now."

"It was a little more than that," I said defensively.

"Wanna talk about it?" *What was it with everyone in my family wanting to talk things over?*

"Nope. Wanna give me a ride to Katy's to get Squib's cover so that he doesn't drown when this rainstorm turns up?"

As I spoke, the rain on the roof starting coming down more heavily. Anders looked out the window with a grimace, then swung his long legs onto the floor and stood up, stretching.

"At your service, as always."

"Thanks bro."

"You owe me," he insisted as we walked out of the front door. "Name your price."

"Hmm. I'll think about it and let you know."

He unlocked the driver's door of his battered old car, and leaned across the front seat to open mine. I shook the raindrops from my hair as I climbed in, settling into the worn out seat and shoving the miscellaneous sports gear and rubbish around with my feet.

"I could clean your car for you."

"Nah," he said as he started the engine. "This favour is gonna be worth way more than that."

The rain eased off slightly as we drove out towards Katy's house, and I crossed my fingers that it wouldn't get too heavy before I could put Squib's cover on him. I hoped it was still where I'd left it, and that Katy hadn't thrown it away or anything. It was so scruffy that she would never mistake it for one of hers, but it was the only one Squib had and he'd be miserable without it.

"It's just up there," I told Anders, pointing out Katy's driveway, and he made the turn smoothly, his old car bumping down the rutted driveway.

As we drove between the trees, I couldn't help remembering the first time I'd ridden Squib down here, when he'd spooked and run away on me. It seemed such a long time ago now. We'd made so much progress since then, and I felt another pang of regret for the way things had turned out.

Anders pulled up in the middle of the yard, and my heart pounded as I saw Lucas standing patiently in the hosing bay. Katy was on a box next to him, pulling his mane, and her head turned towards me as Anders switched off the ignition.

"Wait for me," I told him. "I won't be long."

I took a deep breath and stepped out into the misty rain. After taking a few steps towards the barn, I realised with relief that it was Deb, not Katy. They were the same height with the same length hair, and the misty rain had obscured any other differences.

"AJ!" She looked surprised but happy to see me, and I made myself smile back at her. None of this was her fault.

"Hi. I'm sorry to bother you, but I think I left Squib's cover here, and he's going to need it today."

"Of course." She teased up another length of Lucas's mane, wrapped the small metal comb around it and tugged it out. Lucas stood quietly, his lower lip drooping contentedly. "Do you know where it is?"

I nodded. "Yeah, I'll get it. Thanks."

The cover was exactly where I'd left it, and I lifted it off the hook and folded it over my arm.

"Thank you," I called to Deb as I prepared to step back out into the rain, but she stepped off the box next to Lucas and came over to me.

"Wait up a moment, hon." Her eyes were kind as she looked at me, seeming concerned. "I don't know what happened with you and Katy, and she swears she doesn't know either. But if she's done something to upset you, you can tell me. God knows she does enough to annoy me, so it'll hardly make my head spin."

I bit my lip. "It's nothing. I just…" But I couldn't come up with a reasonable excuse, so I just shrugged.

Deb seemed to realise that I didn't want to talk about it.

"How's Squib?" she asked, changing the subject.

"He's good. His schooling's going heaps better, although he still gets really strong in the canter and tries to run away from me sometimes. But the copper roller is definitely helping." I felt guilty then as I remembered that it still belonged to her. "If you need it back though, let me know," I said quickly, hoping she wouldn't. I'd tried to take it off him a couple of days ago and go back to the snaffle, but he'd reverted right back to crazy uncontrollable Squib and I knew that without it, I'd be back at square one in no time.

Deb shook her head. "You hang onto it for as long as you like," she insisted. "Honestly, there's no rush."

"Thanks. And thanks for all your help with him. I really appreciate it."

"I know," she said with a smile. "We've loved helping you, and we're always here if you need any advice. Just call, or stop by. Anytime."

It was getting harder and harder to leave. I'd thought that I missed being here before, but now that I was standing in their yard, smelling the comforting smells of hay and ponies and the leather and sweat and saddle grease, it was ten times worse.

I looked across the yard at Anders, sitting so patiently in his car. I needed to go. I couldn't make my feet move.

"She wanted to buy Squib. She only made friends with me because she wanted my pony."

The words came out before I could stop them, but I felt better once they were said. Deb's eyebrows shot skyward, and she stared at me for a moment, her brain whirring over the words.

"Katy said that?"

I nodded. "To Hayley, at Feilding."

"Oh, AJ. I'm sure she didn't mean it." I didn't believe her, and Deb could tell, but she kept trying to convince me. "If it makes you feel any better, I would never have agreed to buy him out from under you. Not unless you wanted to sell him, and I'm sure you don't."

I shook my head, and Deb reached out and gave my shoulder a quick squeeze. "I'll talk to Katy about it," she said. "I'm sure it's just a misunderstanding."

"Don't do that," I said quickly. "It doesn't matter."

"Of course it does. You're the best friend she's had in years, and I hate to see you two fall out over such a silly thing…"

I opened my mouth to tell her that it wasn't silly to me when Lucas whinnied, and we both turned to see Katy riding up the driveway on Molly. She looked surprised to see me, and I seized my chance to escape. Clasping the cover tight to my chest, I pulled away from Deb and ran to Anders's car. He started the engine and Katy moved Molly out of the way as he turned the car around and drove us away.

"Where are you, Squib?"

I trudged through the persistent rain, looking for my pony. The cover in my arms was getting heavier by the minute, and my old sneakers soaked up the rain on the ground, making my feet wet. I was right back where I'd started, I realised, going in endless circles without any hope of moving forward.

A flash of bright pink caught my eye, and I had to smile as I walked towards the ponies. Carrie's latest acquisition for Oscar was a bright pink cover, and as silly as it looked on him, it certainly made the ponies easy to spot. Squib was in the middle of the huddle, standing under the trees at the bottom of the gully, and he looked up when I called to him.

I slid down the hill and squelched across the grass towards him, and he watched me come, no longer trying to run away when I approached. He was damp, but the trees had kept the worst of the rain off so far, much to my relief. I threw his cover over him and fastened the straps, then slung my arms around his neck and hugged him. But Squib didn't much like being hugged, and he raised his head and went into reverse. I let him go, then compromised with a quick kiss on his damp muzzle.

"You're the best pony. I'm so lucky to have you," I told him sincerely.

At the top of the hill, I looked back at my pony who was now grazing contentedly. At least *he* was happy. I turned back towards the gate and started walking, then stopped in my tracks and stared in disbelief as Katy came jogging across the paddock towards me.

I had nowhere to go, so I just stood there and watched her approach, wondering what was going to happen now.

"What are you doing here?"

"I came to see you. We have to talk."

"I don't really want to talk to you."

"AJ, come on. I'm sorry. Mum told me what you said, about why you were upset, and you have to know that I didn't mean it."

"You said it," I reminded her.

"Yeah, but only because I was talking to Hayley. If I'd told her that I wasn't interested in Squib, or that I wanted you to train him yourself, then she'd have made fun of me and said stuff about how it was a waste of a good pony. She's so competitive, she can't stand it when people don't go all out to win, all of the time. And after the way she'd been raving on about Tess failing at riding Misty, I didn't want to go down that route with her. I was just trying to shut her up. I didn't know you were listening, and I shouldn't have said it anyway but it just came out. I'm sorry."

I considered her words carefully. "So you don't want to buy Squib?"

Katy was honest. "If you wanted to sell him to me, I'd snap him up in a heartbeat. He's amazing. But I'd never try to talk you into selling him if you didn't want to. In fact, if you said you were selling him tomorrow I'd bust a gut to change your mind. You two are so perfect for each other."

She brushed the wet hair out of her eyes, and I realised that the rain was getting heavier.

"I've been training ponies for years," she continued. "But I've never trained another rider before and it's been so much fun working with you and seeing you improve. Even when you do dumb things like leave the ring before your jump off," she added with a tentative grin.

I pretended to glare at her, but I was having trouble staying mad. I'd missed her so much, and the constant teasing was a part of that.

"Shut up. I only did it once."

"I know, and you won't do it again. You're a fast learner and a hard worker. That's why I like you. And it's been *so* boring at home without you. I forgot how lonely I got before you started hanging around."

"I've been pretty bored too," I admitted.

Katy looked hopeful. "So you'll come back and ride with me again?"

I pretended to consider it for a moment. "Yeah, I guess," I replied with feigned reluctance, although inwardly I was doing a joyful dance.

Katy didn't hold her emotions back, fist-pumping the air triumphantly. "Yes! And you'll bring Squib with you, and keep him at ours, and ride with me every day like we planned?"

"If you'll still have us," I said, grinning back at her.

Katy laughed. "Dude. Just *try* and leave again. I'm going to train you and Squib up to be one of the best show jumping combinations in the country. Just you wait," she promised as we started walking back to the gate, linking her arm through mine and squeezing it tight. "Stick with me, and you two are going to be jumping Grand Prix in no time at all!"

♥

*Also by Kate Lattey*

## PONY JUMPERS

## DARE TO DREAM

## CLEARWATER BAY

For more information, visit nzponywriter.com

Email nzponywriter@gmail.com and sign up to my mailing list for exclusive previews, new releases, giveaways and more!

*Don't miss the next books in the exciting Pony Jumpers series!*

## Pony Jumpers #2
# DOUBLE CLEAR

Katy O'Reilly has grown up on horseback, training promising young ponies under her mother's guidance. Although unable to afford top level show jumpers, she has been fortunate enough to lease two exceptional Grand Prix ponies, and they are both on top of their game and ready to take on the competition.

But just as the season is getting underway, a twist of fate threatens to unravel all of Katy's best laid plans...

♥

## Pony Jumpers #3
# TRIPLE BAR

Susannah Andrews has always been a keen competitor in the sport of show jumping. Spurred on by her parents, she was climbing the Grand Prix leader board with a firm eye on the top prize - until it all fell apart eighteen months ago. Refusing to give up on the sport she loves, and despite continued bullying on the circuit, she has pulled herself back into contention and is determined to prove herself once more.

But when her estranged brother contacts her after a lengthy absence, Susannah faces a tough choice. Can she forgive him for what he did - and if she does, will her parents ever speak to her again?

Pony Jumpers #4
# FOUR FAULTS

Tess Maxwell never really wanted to be a competition rider, and she certainly never wanted to inherit her sister Hayley's difficult Grand Prix pony Misty Magic. But nobody ever listens to what Tess wants, and despite her resolution never to ride Misty again, she finds herself back in the saddle as he continues to tear her confidence to shreds.

After her parents decide that Misty will be sold after Christmas unless Tess changes her mind, she has more to contend with than just surviving the next seven weeks. Because Hayley is determined not to let her beloved pony leave the farm, and she doesn't care what it will take to change her sister's mind…

♥

Pony Jumpers #5
# FIVE STRIDE LINE

AJ is still dreaming of taking her talented pony Squib to the top level of pony show jumping, but she's about to hit some serious roadblocks. Squib has started slipping on the turns, and now her best friend Katy is insisting that AJ needs to put shoes on Squib, instead of letting him jump barefoot as he's always done before. But AJ isn't so sure…

Can AJ achieve her goals without compromising what she feels is best for her pony?

# ACKNOWLEDGEMENTS

I wrote this short novel over a long weekend, as a personal challenge to see how quickly I could write a complete book. Somehow (I'm still not exactly sure how it happened!) I managed to write it in just three days! I went on to write the sequel *Double Clear*, which is told from Katy's point of view, which was followed by *Triple Bar*, told from Susannah's perspective, and then Tess's side of the story came along in *Four Faults* ... and the Pony Jumpers series was on its way, with many more books to come.

If you've read any of my earlier books, you will notice that there were a few familiar faces in *First Fence* – Katy, Susannah and Hayley all featured in my earlier novels *Dare to Dream* and *Dream On*. Each book that I write is connected to the books that have gone before, or that will come after. The show circuit in New Zealand is, after all, a small and close-knit community full of familiar sights, both horse and human!

For more about me and the books I have written, you can visit my website at **nzponywriter.com**, where you can sign up for my mailing list to get new release information, updates and enter giveaways. You can also find me on Facebook as **Kate Lattey - Author** and on Instagram at **@kate_lattey**.

Finally, if you enjoyed reading this book, please consider leaving a review on Amazon or Goodreads to encourage others to give it a try.

# ABOUT THE AUTHOR

Kate Lattey lives in Waikanae, New Zealand and started riding at the age of 10. She was lucky enough to have ponies of her own during her teenage years, and competed regularly in show jumping, eventing and mounted games before finishing college and heading to university, graduating with a Bachelor of Arts in English & Media Studies.

In the years since, she has never been far from horses, and has worked in various jobs including as a livery yard groom in England, a trekking guide in Ireland, a riding school manager in New Zealand, and a summer camp counselor in the USA. It was during her time there that Kate started writing short stories about the camp's horses, which were a huge hit with the campers, and inspired Kate to continue pursuing her passion for writing.

Kate currently owns a Welsh Cob x Thoroughbred gelding named JJ, and competes in show jumping and show hunter competitions, as well as coaching at Pony Club and judging at local events.

She has been reading and writing pony stories ever since she can remember, and has many more yet to come! If you enjoyed this book, check out the rest of the series and her other novels on Amazon, and visit nzponywriter.com to sign up for her mailing list and get information about new and upcoming releases.

# DARE TO DREAM

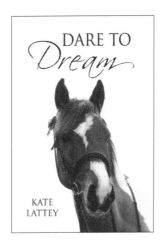

Saying goodbye to the horses they love has become a way of life for Marley and her sisters, who train and sell show jumpers to make their living. Marley has grand ambitions to jump in Pony of the Year, but every good pony she's ever had has been sold out from under her to pay the bills.

Then a half-wild pinto pony comes into her life, and Marley finds that this most unlikely of champions could be the superstar she has always dreamed of. As Marley and Cruise rise quickly to the top of their sport, it seems as though her dream might come true after all.

But her family is struggling to make ends meet, and as the countdown to Pony of the Year begins, Marley is forced to face the possibility of losing the pony she has come to love more than anything else in the world.

Can Marley save the farm she loves, without sacrificing the pony she can't live without?

# DREAM ON

*"Nobody has ever tried to understand this pony.
Nobody has ever been on her side. Until now.
She needs you to fight for her, Marley. She needs you to love her."*

Borderline Majestic was imported from the other side of the world to bring her new owners fame and glory, but she is almost impossible to handle and ride. When the pony lands her rider in intensive care, it is up to Marley to prove that the talented mare is not dangerous - just deeply misunderstood.

Can Marley dare to fall in love again to save Majestic's life?

This much-anticipated sequel to *Dare to Dream* was a Top 20 Kindle Book Awards Semi-Finalist in 2015.

Clearwater Bay #1
# FLYING CHANGES

When Jay moves from her home in England to live with her estranged father in rural New Zealand, it is only his promise of a pony of her own that convinces her to leave her old life behind and start over in a new country.

Change doesn't come easily at first, and Jay makes as many enemies as she does friends before she finds the perfect pony, who seems destined to make her dreams of show jumping success come true.

But she soon discovers that training her own pony is not as easy as she thought it would be, and her dream pony is becoming increasingly unmanageable and difficult to ride.

Can Jay pull it all together, or has she made the biggest mistake of her life?

# AGAINST THE CLOCK

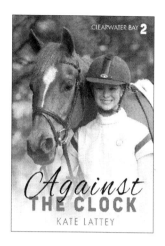

It's a new season and a new start for Jay and her wilful pony Finn, but their best laid plans are quickly plagued by injuries, arguments and rails that just won't stay in their cups. And when her father introduces her to his new girlfriend, Jay can't help wondering if her life will ever run according to plan.

While her friends battle with their own families and Jay struggles to define hers, it is only her determination to bring out the best in her pony that keeps her going. But after overhearing a top rider say that Finn's potential is being hampered by her incompetent rider, Jay is besieged by doubts in her own ability...and begins to wonder whether Finn would be better off without her.

Can Jay bear to give up on her dreams, even if it's for her pony's sake?

Made in the USA
San Bernardino, CA
04 May 2018